OBSESSED

OBSESSED

EROTIC ROMANCE
FOR WOMEN

EDITED BY
RACHEL KRAMER BUSSEL

FOREWORD BY
CARIDAD PIÑEIRO

CLEiS
PRESS

Published in the United States by Cleis Press, Inc., 2246 Sixth Street, Berkeley, California 94710.

Printed in the United States.
Cover design: Scott Idleman/Blink
Cover photograph: Jurgen Reisch/Getty Images
Text design: Frank Wiedemann

First Edition.
10 9 8 7 6 5 4 3 2 1

Trade paper ISBN: 978-1-57344-718-8
E-book ISBN: 978-1-57344-739-3

Contents

FOREWORD: BEHIND THE MASK OF OBSESSION

Caridad Piñeiro

Obsession.

It's a word bandied about in television commercials trying to sell you an assortment of items. People admit to being obsessed about everything from foods to movies to books, not really understanding the true meaning of obsession.

In its most extreme forms, obsession becomes the master, overtaking heart, mind and soul with no thought of reason. It can enslave when there is no way to end the compulsion for some one or some thing, or it can liberate when the obsession is satisfied and brings enlightenment.

As a writer of paranormal romances and romantic suspense, I play with the idea of obsession in its various forms, using it to create characters and stories that engage the reader emotionally and bring them to the edge of their seats as they root for the characters they have come to love. From the moment of first flirtation to complete fulfillment in the happily-ever-after, obsession lies beneath the surface, driving lovers to satisfaction both physically and emotionally. But also keep in mind that obsession lies just as powerfully in the hearts of every vampire, demon or villain as they, too, lose control and are enslaved in the struggle to possess blood or a soul or power regardless of the price to be paid.

The women writers in this wonderful anthology likewise create stories and characters that will connect with you and have you following them along their journeys to satisfaction and enlightenment. The stories will also challenge you to walk along the edge where control wobbles and it takes self-awareness to not lose oneself.

The writers in *Obsessed* understand one other powerful thing about obsession, namely that in its most satisfying forms, obsession is also about knowledge, which brings power in a myriad of ways: The power to give yourself to someone else with complete trust or to understand the emotions that make you seek perfection. The power to rip away the mask that you wear for the outside world so that you can display the real you, or to put on a mask and become something that you are not.

The many talented writers in *Obsessed* demonstrate their understanding of the nuances of obsession from its beginning steps of fascination to finding completion to even skirting the edge before one loses control, only to snatch it back and become master again instead of slave, seizing control of heart, mind and body, gaining knowledge about the pleasure to be found in the sexual and sensual experiences they undertake as they satisfy their obsessions.

How does obsession begin?

It can be born from something quite simple, such as a fascination with an object that seems to be out of place, like the hook in Ariel Graham's "Hooked."

How does obsession grow?

A first taste of something forbidden or delectable can linger in one's memory, becoming larger with every passing day until a second taste is demanded. A one-night stand with a boss makes a normally professional woman toss aside convention for "One Night in Paris," by Kayla Perrin, while another woman snaps up a chance for adventure in the Big Apple in "Raindrops and Rooftops," by Elizabeth Coldwell.

How does obsession end?

Maybe it doesn't. Maybe even in the fulfillment there is need that lives on, keeping alive the light of love and exploration, as demonstrated in Rachel Kramer Bussel's heartfelt look at married love in "I Want to Hold Your Hand."

When does obsession enslave?

Tattoos, burlesque, naughty underwear and even hurricane-force winds all push women to the fine edge of control in stories by Andrea Dale, Logan Belle, Louisa Harte and Teresa Noelle Roberts. In each story, daring women explore the needs of their bodies and hearts in order to understand what forces bring them both emotional and physical obsession.

Daring women are present in each story of this anthology. They are daring because each of them is willing to explore their needs and find ways to satisfy them. They are women who are up to the challenge and open to new possibilities.

They are women like you, ready to explore their obsessions and by doing so, gain power, knowledge and satisfaction—maybe even a new awareness of something previously unknown.

Enjoy this sensual and sexual journey offered by the women in *Obsessed*. Maybe when you're finished you'll take the time to take your own journey.

INTRODUCTION

The women in *Obsessed* show their passion for their lovers in all kinds of ways. For some it's about indulging in acts of daring, for others it's about letting go of their preconceived notions of propriety and going where their bodies tell them.

In many of these stories, communication, the touchstone of advice about good relationships, is missing in some key way, whether it's the almost-divorced couple in "Aftershocks" by Bella Andre who finally, during an earthquake, confess their deepest desires, or the one-time lovers in "Silent Treatment" by Donna George Storey who find plenty to say with their bodies at a silent retreat. In "Then," Emerald explores what happens after a woman confesses to her boyfriend just how much she lusts after another man. They push the boundaries of their relationship and the boundaries of their trust in each other—another theme of this book.

Charlotte Stein paints a portrait of a "Loser" who manages to capture the attention of the narrator—and keep it by impressing her with his ardent desire. Stein writes, "He does little things, like when I stop him saying words like those with my mouth on his, he brings his hands up to cup my face. Other guys don't cup my face. And he does it as though he wants to keep me as close as possible, so he can fully concentrate on my mouth and the way it moves and how much tongue I'm giving him at any given time."

Obsessed is not about obsession for a new purse or a new car or a new perfume. It's not even about the obsessiveness of a crush, the kind of panting lust that cycles over and over itself with no end in sight. Instead, *Obsessed* is about the way a lover can get under your skin, can drive you crazy with lust as well as so many other emotions—love, longing, hunger, anger, confusion. Are there happy endings here? Yes, there are, but they are not always the happy endings you'd expect. These stories sizzle with the kind of obsession that is fueled by our deepest desires, the ones that hold couples together, the ones that haunt us and don't let go. Whether experiencing just-blooming passions, rekindled sparks or reinvented relationships, these lovers put the object of their obsession first. They don't always do what's rational or proper; instead, they chase their dreams, as in Kayla Perrin's "One Night in Paris," across the world and across the landscape of their lovers' bodies.

I hope *Obsessed* speaks to the part of you that knows what it's like to do anything for the right person, to bare yourself body and soul in the hope that once stripped to your most secret self, you will be rewarded with someone who sees you for who you truly are. With these nineteen stories, though, you don't have to hope—I can tell you now that these gutsy heroines find men who know exactly how to treat their wild, hungry hearts. How they get there is yours to savor.

Rachel Kramer Bussel
New York City

SILENT TREATMENT

Donna George Storey

I came to this place to hear myself think.

Which meant forty-eight hours without speaking or being spoken to, give or take a couple of hushed interviews with the meditation instructor. They call it a "silent" retreat, but the first time I treated myself to a weekend getaway at this austere-yet-comfortable mountain spa last spring, my ears were flooded with sound: birdsong, the swoosh of the breeze through new leaves, the faint drone of an airplane slicing through the sky. And then, hesitantly, like a seedling pushing through soil, the sound of that deeper voice hiding low in my chest, the voice that was mostly silenced by the noise of the city.

I liked what it had to tell me.

Now it was October, and I found myself craving pure quietude with a sensual ache in my belly that I usually reserved for a slice of apricot-chocolate torte with freshly whipped cream at my local Viennese pastry shop.

Due to a last-minute conference call at work, I missed the

reception where you introduce yourself to the other participants before all human interaction recedes to quiet smiles and quick nods of greeting. I'd heard it all last spring. We were all escaping hectic lives, seeking our true inner voice. However, I didn't want to miss the opening meditation session, so I made a makeshift dinner out of an apple and a protein bar as I wove my car along the narrow road snaking up to the retreat center. Dusk had fallen by the time I arrived. The windows of the central hall glowed like elvish lanterns through the trees.

I checked in and got my room key—all in mime, changed into my yoga clothes and hurried over to the hall, leaves crunching beneath my feet, my breath hissing frosty puffs into the autumn darkness. The shoji door rumbled rudely as I slid it open. A dark-haired man seated in half-lotus in the last row glanced back at me, his expression more curiosity than annoyance. Still I felt a blush color my cheeks.

It took another moment for me to realize I knew him.

The blush turned to pure fire.

Of all the silent retreats, in all the towns, in all the world, he had to walk into mine.

Oh, I *knew* him all right. His name was Stephen Rejebian, and ironically he'd been much in my thoughts the last time I came on retreat, until that wise woman within counseled me to let it pass and move on. I'll admit I was obsessed with him at the time, but as far as heartbreaks go, it was a fairly mild fissure. Three promising get-togethers gave me no claim over him, even if our last date was also the best first-time sex I'd ever had in my life. Sometimes I still flashed on the intoxicating pleasure of our sweaty *pas de deux*, my legs gripping his bucking hips as I ground my clit on his belly, his tireless lips and fingers tug-tug-tugging on my stiff, sensitive nipples. Stephen sure knew how to make a woman scream. We had a repeat performance scheduled for the next weekend, but he'd canceled by text message: A sudden family commitment. He was sorry and would be in touch soon.

I hadn't heard from him since.

Willing my hands to remain steady, I plucked a round cushion from the cabinet by the door and took my place at the very back of the room, a safe distance behind Stephen. I'd seen the mutual flicker of recognition in his eyes, the way his lips fought between a smile and a frown. Of course he wasn't allowed to say anything to me even if he'd wanted to, but I thought I noticed a new tension in his back.

Taking a cleansing breath, I studied him coolly as if he were nothing more than a picture in an old photo album. He was thinner than when I'd known him. His arms were taut and ropey with veins, his shapely ass looked a bit narrower. The fingers, however, were as deliciously thick and sturdy as before.

In spite of it all, I still wanted to fuck him.

I swallowed down the laughter bubbling in my chest. The universe sure had a sense of humor. No doubt poor Stephen hadn't expected to run into a ghost from his past either. Still I had to look on the bright side. Our common vow of silence would spare any awkward greetings or explanations until Sunday afternoon, and I didn't plan to stick around afterward to deal with that. If we made eye contact again, I'd treat him with the same beatific calm as I did my other fellow seekers—with a cordial nod at morning yoga, a distant smile if we crossed paths at the tea urn during break.

When the chime sounded at the end of the session, I rose immediately and slipped out of the hall to my room. Wrapped in a soft Japanese quilt, I listened to the wind rattling the leaves, the oratory of an owl. Alone in here, my inner voice was willing to admit it—being dropped cold by Stephen after he'd "had his way with me" had hurt, and the wound still ached faintly. But this was a chance to show *myself* how strong and resilient I was in the face of life's inevitable disappointments. I felt my jaw soften, my chest expand until a part of me—the real me—stepped out of my body to float in the freedom of silence. That slippery naked dance with Stephen, the lack of chemistry with the guy I was now dating, the whole long drama that was my ex-husband—all concerns of the flesh were suddenly the dream now.

I fell asleep feeling oddly warm, as if I were wrapped up in strong, loving arms.

For most of Saturday, fate decided to be kind. Stephen didn't show up for the yoga class at dawn. He was already seated at the far end of the hall during morning gathering, and since I'd taken my green tea and steel-cut oatmeal out to the terrace, I didn't even see him at breakfast. Our gazes met briefly as we all headed out for walking meditation, and I responded exactly as planned—with a faint smile of universal good will, which he returned in kind.

I was beginning to think he really was nothing more than a phantom of my own imagination, a reminder of the folly and emotional cacophony of the "real" world. That is, until I reported to the kitchen for after-dinner cleanup duty, my assigned work service for the weekend. Stephen and a grandmotherly older woman were already there, studying a notebook describing our tasks. I swallowed down the panic twisting my stomach and joined them, my shoulders back, my chin high. Stephen stepped aside for me. My pulse racing, I read the instructions quickly. One of us was supposed to refill the hot water urns, replenish the tea supplies and lay out the evening snacks. The other two would gather any abandoned dishes, then wipe down the tables and sweep the floor. The older woman pointed at the first job, her eyebrows raised in a question. Stephen and I both nodded.

Then we looked at each other.

His eyes almost leaped out at me, and he instinctively parted his lips to speak.

Grinning in spite of myself, I shook my head. It took everything I had in me not to touch my finger to his lips and say: *Hush.*

He blushed, but kept his gaze fixed on me.

It was, in fact, the only way we could speak.

In the almost palpable weight of our silence, that prickling warmth of desire suddenly sprang to life *down there*. Stephen was glad to see me. There was no question about that. And he wanted to express something else with those bottomless amber eyes: Apology. A faint sorrow. And—no mistake about it—hot, smoking desire.

Flustered, but still smiling, I reached for the broom. Without a word, he gallantly slipped it from my hands—I suppose it was the dirtier job—and I scooped up a cleaning rag and spray bottle of eco-friendly disinfectant solution for the table cleanup. I tackled the first table, and he began sweeping near the door, but we soon fell into a companionable routine. I'd wipe off the table with long, gliding strokes, then we'd both move the chairs. He'd sweep underneath, while I took on the next table or two with my washrag, then we'd collaborate on chair duty again. Although I once caught him eyeing my butt appreciatively as I bent over a long table, working together in silence seemed to bring us together in a calm, relaxing rhythm.

As I wiped away crumbs and lifted chairs carefully to preserve the quiet serenity of the place, I decided I might just hang around a bit the next afternoon, in case Stephen wanted to talk. And if he didn't, we'd had this, which even my inner voice admitted was a good thing all on its own.

After putting away the cleaning supplies, we both lingered in the dining hall. I pretended I wanted some chamomile tea to take back to the room. He busied himself wrapping up a homemade granola bar in a cloth napkin. Without a word—naturally—we left together. He held the door for me as I stepped out into the clear, cold evening, the crescent moon hanging low like a Venetian gondola on the eastern horizon.

We both paused to admire the night sky, then I felt him turn to look down at me. I caught my breath. I could swear I heard words through his unmoving lips. *It's a beautiful night. You're beautiful. There's a reason we're together here.*

Or is that only what I wanted to hear?

Did it matter? We were in a place where the real me decided what happened, not the voice of common sense yammering, "You should make him work harder for forgiveness after what he did," and "If he fucks you over again, you have only yourself to blame." I reached out and brushed his hand, nothing more than an unspoken way to reassure him that I forgave his long, hurtful silence. I wasn't surprised when he wrapped his fingers around mine and squeezed.

But my own response shook me. My pussy contracted like a fist, as if he'd touched me there instead, and a jolt of electric pleasure made my nipples so hard I was almost afraid they'd poke holes in my shirt.

I guess I did still want to fuck him.

My next impulse was to drag him into the woods and do something terribly rash and forbidden: talk. But my inner voice counseled a safer option. I gave his hand two quick tugs, then stepped toward my room with a meaningful glance over my shoulder.

He followed.

Fortunately, I'd kept my quarters neat, as seemed fitting for a purifying retreat. I switched on the shoji lamp by the futon to the night-light option. A pale golden light filled the room. The last time we'd made love was in darkness, but this time I wanted to see everything.

Our eyes met in a question. *What next?*

We answered in unison by stepping forward into each other's arms. The first kiss was chaste, his mouth soft, the friction of his five o'clock shadow on my soft skin bracing and, yes, incredibly arousing. I opened my lips to him and took in his hot tongue.

Tell me. Help me understand.

He let out a soft moan.

I pulled away, smiling, and this time I did put my finger to his lips. In the privacy of my room, we might have allowed ourselves some discreet whispering. But Stephen had closed himself off from me with silence. It seemed only right that silence would open up the way between us again.

We fell onto the bed, twined together like teenagers, our greedy kisses wandering over each other's lips, cheeks, eyelids, necks. I could feel his hard-on through the yielding fabric of his meditation pants. I myself was already shamelessly sopping wet, and I rocked against his thigh like an animal in heat.

With a sharp exhalation, he yanked up my shirt and unclasped my bra. He took one taut nipple in his mouth and rubbed the other between his fingers as if he were caressing fine silk.

I squirmed, pressing my lips so tightly together I thought I might draw blood. Out in the real world, I'd be moaning my head off by now, but the cries trapped in my chest made the pleasure almost unbearably exquisite. My skin was slick with sweat, and the pulsing in my belly threatened to burst through my ribs. Desperate for release, I wriggled away and sat up. His eyes widened in confusion at my apparent rejection, but he grinned approvingly when I shucked off my shirt and bra and tossed them across the floor. Together we slithered out of our pants and underwear. I leered at his bobbing erection. *Nice.*

He gave me a mischievous smile, and we burrowed under the covers, rubbing against each other desperately, as if our bodies missed each other more than our minds would admit. Then, in one quick movement, he rolled on top. I wiggled my thighs open and dry-humped his stomach. He suckled me, eyes closed in ecstasy as if my nipples were the most delectable dish he'd ever eaten. I pushed my swollen cunt lips against his hard belly, the voice in my head almost screaming.

Fuck me, oh, god, I need you inside.

As if in reply, he stopped and looked at me intently.

I'd love to fuck you, but I don't have a condom. Though I know another way to make you very happy.

How could I protest as he slid under the blanket and parted my thighs? I'd gotten a good sampling of his tongue tricks last time, though I'd held myself back for the main course. But this time I surrendered completely to the flicks and flutters of his tongue. When he began to pinch my nipples rhythmically, a choked moan seeped through my lips. In spite of my body's betrayal, I was determined to maintain my vow. But it wasn't easy. My breath came in gasps. My pussy was so wet, it made a telltale slurping sound beneath his lips.

He was definitely speaking my language. My thighs began to tremble, and my head thrashed back and forth on the pillow as if I were being slapped.

How can you let him do this after what happened last time?

The words in my head were faint, far away. Was that my real voice? But in the next instant my doubts were blotted out by a flurry of lashes from Stephen's merciless tongue.

Go for the pleasure. Pleasure heals.

The pulsing heat in my cunt throbbed and swelled, filling my whole torso with a white-hot scream. Yet only a soft "Ah," escaped my lips as my hips jerked rhythmically. Stephen grabbed my ass and rode my climax with me to the finish.

Afterward he held me until my breath slowed and the sweat cooled. Then I rose up on one elbow, cocked an eyebrow.

He grinned and shook his head.

That one was on me.

I almost insisted, because I was hungry for him. I wanted his cock in my mouth, wanted to show him what my tongue could do with the gift of silence. Besides, all the rules said you had to leave your man satisfied.

But I had to admit that there was something right about leaving this unfinished, open to possibility. And he did owe me, after all.

Stephen drew me into his arms. The steady beating of his heart was as soothing as a lullaby.

I fell asleep in his arms.

When I opened my eyes, my room was filled with pearl-gray light. Stephen was still beside me. He had already been awake, I wasn't sure for how long, but he turned his head to me and smiled. We kissed again; not the hungry, desperate probing of the night before, but a lingering meeting of lips that promised more.

As he left to go back to his room, his eyebrows lifted in a final question.

I nodded.

Only when he was gone did I start to worry. When we talked after the retreat, it could get awkward. Because he'd have to have a very good excuse for what he did, and he'd damned well better apologize.

Quiet now. He's already said everything you needed to hear.

I recognized that voice, so calm and resonant, the one I came to this place to hear.

Smiling, I took a deep breath and surrendered to the silence.

ONE NIGHT IN PARIS

Kayla Perrin

This is crazy.

That's the thought that flits into my mind as I sit in the lobby of the Marriott Paris Neuilly, a beautiful hotel in the tree-filled residential neighborhood of Neuilly-sur-Seine near downtown Paris, France. I have come here on a whim, flown from Dallas on a red-eye flight so I can be here in the City of Light for one night. A completely irrational plan, I know. But my obsession has forced me to finally take action.

And my sense is that here in Paris, away from the office, is exactly where my utmost desire can be fulfilled.

That is, *if* he wants to see me.

He being Aaron Taylor, Chief Financial Officer of Creighton and Taylor Capital. He's a venture capitalist, one of those money guys who provide funding to get startup businesses off the ground.

And I, Vivian Sinclair, am his executive assistant. Which is how I know not only exactly where he is right now, but the suite he is staying in here at this Marriott hotel.

I know because I took care of all the travel arrangements.

And I'm here because...well, because I've spent the last two years obsessing over Aaron Taylor. He has consumed so much of my thoughts, even when I've been dating. There isn't a day he comes into the office when I don't feel a rush of lust as I stare at his killer body. His tight butt, his broad back, his muscular thighs and his all-around beautifully toned physique. I especially love to watch him slip out of his blazer and see the way his shoulder blades move beneath his dress shirt. Aaron used to play professional football for the Dallas Cowboys, which is how he developed his incredibly sexy body—and how he earned the cash to start his company with a fellow NFL player.

I've been Aaron's executive assistant for three years. And I've been lusting after him from the very first day. But my lust intensified two years ago, when we fell into bed together for one passionate night.

Drawing in a deep breath to calm my nerves, I glance outside at the overcast October day. The fall colors are in full bloom, with the tree leaves a myriad of oranges, yellows and reds. Then I look at my watch for the umpteenth time. It is just after three Paris time.

I've been waiting here in the lobby for a good hour. I'm not sure why. No, that's not true. I know exactly why I'm in the lobby as opposed to up in Aaron's suite. I've had this moment planned out in my mind for three months, ever since I first learned Aaron might be traveling to Paris. In my fantasies, I'm sitting here on a lobby sofa as I am right now, and Aaron enters the hotel. At first he doesn't see me. He's tired from a long day of negotiations. But I stand, wearing my red, patent-leather, knee-high boots and my black patent-leather coat. It is then that he notices me, and his eyes light up. A surge of lust passes from him to me, instantly turning me on. Then we head upstairs and I finally get relief for my turbulent desire, which has been out of control ever since that first and only time I slept with him.

Sure, I could easily be strategically placed on the king-sized bed in his suite. But I want to see Aaron as he enters the hotel. I want to be able to gauge his reaction to my being here instead of simply shocking him when he enters his suite and finds me there.

Besides, I am here in Paris for this one night for the fantasy—not just the night of hardcore fucking I envision. I want the seduction.

So part of my sitting here in the lobby is because I want to sexually torture Aaron as we ride the elevator up to his suite. When I loosen the ties on my coat and give him a glimpse of my naked cleavage, I want him to *want* to take me in the elevator, long before we even reach the suite's double doors.

I am not really paying much attention to the magazine in my hands, which I'm holding so that I look like I'm occupied and not like a woman sitting around waiting for the moment when she can fuck her boss. I feel a nervous energy causing my hands to tremble slightly. And I also feel an excitement that's making my pussy throb.

There's a tall, attractive bald man working at the front desk who has glanced my way several times since I've been sitting in the lobby. I first noticed him checking me out when I arrived at the hotel and got my keys to Aaron's suite. I'm sure he was surprised to see me come back downstairs a short while after check-in, dressed in my shiny red boots and black leather coat. But given the number of times he's been looking at me, he was pleasantly surprised.

I cross one leg over the other, doing my best to ensure that

I don't expose myself. Beneath my coat, I am not wearing any underwear.

The heat of the man's gaze burns my skin, and I shoot him a quick look. He grins. I'm not sure what he thinks. That I'm a prostitute, perhaps? I know that my outfit oozes sex appeal. Or perhaps he thinks I'm hoping to get lucky with a random stranger.

"Come on, Aaron," I whisper. "Where are you?"

I stand, debating whether or not to go up to the room. I'm beginning to feel self-conscious. It isn't just the hotel clerk staring at me. There are some businessmen sitting at the nearby bar also staring in my direction, not even trying to make a secret of it.

My gaze wanders from the three men toward the hotel's glass front doors. And suddenly, there he is.

Aaron.

My heart slams into my rib cage as my legs go still. I literally feel a rush that makes my head swoon.

Either my fantasy is about to begin...or a nightmare will ensue.

Aaron is loosening his tie as he walks, his gait powerful and sexy. Has any man looked more amazing in a suit? Tailored perfectly to fit his broad shoulders and those amazing muscular thighs...he looks, wearing it, like an Adonis sculpted from dark, delicious chocolate.

I feel the same primal urge I've felt ever since that one and only time we slept together, something he'd called a "mistake" because he'd been engaged at the time.

But he's not engaged now, and I haven't been able to stop thinking about the only man who easily gave me multiple orgasms. I've pleasured myself while thinking of him many, many times—but it simply isn't enough anymore.

At first he doesn't see me. But either he senses my gaze or

catches a glimpse of my sexy outfit, and his eyes raise to meet mine.

I watch, not breathing. Everything is riding on how he reacts.

He slows. His eyes narrow. I see confusion and disbelief on his face, as though he is questioning what he is really seeing.

And then: "Viv?"

"Hi," I say.

Aaron steps toward me. He's not smiling, but he doesn't look disappointed. "What are you doing here? Is there a prob—"

The words die on his lips as his eyes sweep over me from head to toe. The coat. The boots. The makeup. Suddenly, he gets it.

"I needed to see you," I tell him honestly. Again, I notice that the clerk is eyeing me, and I am done being a showpiece in this hotel lobby.

I am ready to get naked and fuck.

Aaron says nothing, and I'm not sure what he's thinking. But I start to walk, and he falls into step beside me. Together we head to the elevator. Thankfully, when it opens, we are the only ones to enter.

"Viv—"

I ease forward, placing my fingers on his lips. "No. Don't say anything. Let me speak first." The elevator door closes, and suddenly I am doing something I have only been brave enough to do in my dreams. I am taking Aaron's hand in mine and placing it beneath the hem of my coat, trailing it upward until his finger touches my naked vagina.

His eyes widen in shock.

"Shhh," I say. I don't want him to utter words of caution, or worse, to reject me. I came all this way to fulfill a fantasy and I will not be denied. "All I want is today. One night in Paris with you."

And I mean it, every word. Oh, sure, I'd like a whole lot more of Aaron—endless nights of pleasure—but if this is all I can get of him, I'll take it gladly. I *need* to be with this man, even if there is no guarantee of a tomorrow.

He is staring at me with a look of surprised awe on his face, and my breath catches, fearing that he is going to reject me, after all I've done to set this up. But Aaron doesn't remove his hand from my pussy. He lets it linger there, and my clitoris throbs against his finger.

And then he moves his finger over me, exploring my sex, and the charge of pleasure is so intense, I gasp.

"Yes, Aaron…"

The elevator stops all too quickly, and I know I should step backward, separate myself from him. Aaron knows it, too, but when he begins to move his hand, I tighten my thighs around it, needing more of him.

The elevator door opens, and I glance over my shoulder to see if anyone is getting on at the penthouse floor. Fortunately, no one is there to see me and Aaron in this compromising position.

Aaron's gaze flits upward, and I follow his gaze to the small camera in the corner of the elevator. "We'd better head to the room."

We get off the elevator, and Aaron walks briskly to the end of the hall and the double doors that lead to the presidential suite. I produce the key before he can and slip it into the slot on the door.

I step into the suite ahead of Aaron, and when I hear the door click shut, I turn to face him. I immediately begin to loosen the tie on my coat, then undo the buttons from the top.

"I can't believe you came here," Aaron says.

"I needed to see you." Three buttons undone now, and my breasts are almost fully exposed. "You're like a fever I can't shake. Ever since that time we were together, I haven't been able to stop thinking about you. And now that you're not with Chelsea anymore, there's no reason we can't..." My buttons completely undone, I spread the sides of my coat and expose my nakedness. I let his eyes wander over me, drink in my nudity.

"I want to fuck you. I *need* to."

And then I move toward him.

He's erect. I can see his cock straining against his pinstriped tailored pants. I reach for it, run my finger along the entire length.

"I want to make you come," I tell him. "Right now." I undo his belt. "You have no idea how badly I want your hard cock in my mouth."

A sort of shaky chuckle escapes from Aaron's throat. I'm certain I've just said the words that all men would love to hear: *I'm giving you myself, no strings attached.*

I loosen Aaron's pants, then drag them down his thighs. He is wearing black boxers, and I make quick work of pushing them down his legs. For a moment, all I can do is stare at the magnificent sight of his cock. It's large and thick and as hard as a slab of granite.

Mewling my delight, I give Aaron a gentle shove until his back is pressed against the wall beside the door, and then I drop onto my haunches before him.

I look up at him. His lips are parted as he stares down at me in anticipation. I keep my eyes locked with his as I run my fingernails up his inner thighs; as I massage his scrotum; as I take his cock in my right hand and guide it into my open mouth.

Oh, my god...the scent of him, the feel, the taste... He is exactly as I have remembered in every one of my fantasies. I suck him hard, take him deep, getting wetter every time I hear him groan. I pump his shaft to heighten his pleasure, wanting to control him, make him remember this blow job long after we have gone back to our boss/employee relationship.

I want to make *him* obsess over me.

Slipping his fingers into my hair, he grips fistfuls of my short tresses. "God," he utters. "Damn it, Viv—that feels fucking amazing."

Massaging his balls, I take him deeper. I want to make him come, and come hard. But the next thing I know, Aaron is urging me upward and planting his lips on mine. He slips his fingers out of my hair and moves them beneath my coat, where he fondles my breasts. He flicks his thumbs back and forth over my nipples until I am moaning into his mouth. Then his right hand goes lower and covers my pussy.

His fingers begin to explore immediately, urgent and needy. He spreads my folds, circles my clit over and over again. As he groans in satisfaction, he pushes a finger into my pussy. Gripping his shoulders, I emit a shuddery moan. Then he eases another finger inside of me, pushing both of them as far into me as they can go.

"Fuck, Viv, your pussy feels amazing. Soft and wet and oh, god!"

"Another finger," I beg him. "Please..."

Aaron adds another digit and finger-fucks me wildly. As he does, he lowers his face to one of my breasts and draws my nipple into his mouth. Prickles of pleasure assault my body. He grazes my nipple with his teeth and bites it gently before trilling my hard peak with his hot, ravenous tongue.

My body is on sensory overload. For two long years, I have waited for this moment. Dreamed about it.

Obsessed about it.

"I want to eat you," he rasps, and I almost come at the words. Two years hasn't been nearly long enough for me to forget the skill with which this man ate my pussy. No one else has even come close to matching his abilities.

Aaron drags my coat off my shoulders and lets it fall to the floor. Now I'm standing before him totally naked—except for the boots. His eyes darken with desire, and I see his cock flinch. Oh, yes. He wants me as much as I want him.

Aaron is strong, and he easily lifts me. I lock my legs around his waist. My lips seek his, and we neck hungrily as he kicks off his shoes and pants, and then carries me to the bedroom.

There, he eases me onto the bed. His mouth moves from my lips to my neck, where he flicks his tongue over my heated skin in broad strokes. His tongue travels from my neck through the valley between my breasts, down past my rib cage, and dips into my belly button before heading toward my pussy. But suddenly Aaron pulls back, and my body instantly misses his hot tongue.

He settles his face between my thighs. I look down at him, wanting to witness the moment his mouth covers my clitoris. But he doesn't give me what I want. Not immediately. Instead, his eyes feast on my pussy, and the raw lust I see in their depths makes my need reach a fever pitch.

"Oh, man," he utters, as though the sight of my pussy is the most beautiful thing in the world. Finally, he touches me, stroking my clit with his fingers. I mewl in delight. Next, he kisses my clit—a quick peck. Not nearly enough. He strokes it again. Kisses it again. I whimper, the sound telling him that I need more.

And then he opens his mouth wide and brings it down on my pussy. His tongue circles my most sensitive spot, causing the sweetest heat.

Aaron laps at me hungrily, his grunts of pleasure telling me he is as excited as I am. He eases one finger inside of me, and another, and then sucks my clit steadily while fingering me relentlessly. He pleases me with his tongue, his teeth and his fingers until I can't take it anymore. My orgasm builds quickly and tears through me with extreme force. I arch my back and grip the bedsheets. Aaron suckles me harder, eating my throbbing pussy as I come in waves of pleasure.

"Aaron!" I cry. "Oh, my god...oh, my god!"

He continues to suck and lick my clit until I'm whimpering, the pleasure almost too intense. Finally, he eases his face up my body, stroking and licking my nipples before he gets to my lips.

His tongue ravages my mouth the way he just ravaged my pussy.

"Climb on top of me," Aaron demands when he tears his lips from mine.

He rolls onto his back, pulling me with him. I straddle him quickly, reaching for his cock as I do.

Our gazes lock, and a rush of warmth shoots through me. Not just a sexual rush, but something more. Because I suddenly get the sense that this means something to Aaron. That it isn't just about fucking.

"Ride me, baby."

I slide down onto his cock, and my eyes flutter shut as I savor the feel of the man I have fantasized over for years deep inside of me again.

"Nothing feels as good as your cock, Aaron. Nothing."

Our movements are slow at first, but we quickly gain momentum. Soon, I am riding him hard and gasping not just from the pleasure, but from the magnitude of my feelings for him.

Who am I kidding? My obsession for Aaron Taylor is about more than my sexual lust.

It's about love.

Each hard thrust of his cock reaches a place deep inside of me, beyond more than simply physical pleasure.

I don't want this to stop. I want to fuck him until we both can't move a single muscle.

This time when I come, it is with a force so powerful, my body tingles with delicious prickles from head to toe. I cry out Aaron's name, suddenly knowing that even though I wanted one night in Paris with him, it won't be enough.

Not even close.

Aaron grips my hips as he comes, and I tighten my vaginal walls around his cock, hoping to draw out every ounce of his orgasm.

When his climax subsides, I fall forward onto his body and rest my face in the crook of his neck. His dress shirt is damp with perspiration. His penis is still inside of me, exactly where I want it to be.

As I lie on top of him, enjoying the feel of my soft body against his hard one, I wonder for the first time what's going to come next. This isn't ground I covered in my fictional fantasy.

We are silent for a long while. Then Aaron reaches for my face, guides it above his.

At first I think he is going to kiss me, but instead, he speaks.

"Wow." He grins. "Seriously, Viv. Wow."

I chuckle softly. It's a sentiment I share. "I've waited a long time to do this with you again," I confess. "I know the first time was…complicated…and I didn't want to put you in that position again. Now, neither of us has to feel guilty."

"The last thing I'm feeling is guilty," Aaron tells me.

"Good." I stroke his face. I can't help showing him tenderness, even though it's probably best to keep some emotional distance. "I'm glad."

Several beats of silence pass. Aaron is looking at me with an expression I can't read.

"What?" I finally ask.

"You say you want only one night." He pauses briefly. "But who says we can't continue this when...when we get back to Dallas?" he finishes, trailing a finger down the length of my back.

I stare at him. "Are you serious?"

Slowly, he nods. "Why not? I'm single, you're single. We can see where this leads. No pressure. But lots of great sex as we figure it out."

After my years of craving this man, this is more than I ever expected. The best possible news.

Because now I have hope.

"You *are* serious," I say.

"You think I've forgotten our first time? Why do you think it didn't work out with Chelsea? I knew it wasn't fair to marry her when I couldn't stop thinking about that night of incredible sex...with you."

My lips part in surprise. "You never said anything."

"Because I didn't want to blur the lines of our working relationship. But damn." He squeezes my ass with both of his hands. "You've pretty much shot that to hell."

"You didn't complain," I tell him, with what is no doubt a goofy smile on my face.

"No. I didn't. And I won't complain the next time."

"No?" I ask, and gyrate my pussy over his cock.

"No." The word is a low, guttural sound.

I continue to gyrate against him and feel an immense thrill when he begins to get hard again.

"Good," I whisper, and begin to unbutton his shirt. I want him completely naked. "Because I am so ready for round two."

Aaron grins, then pulls my head down and kisses me long and hard, officially starting the second round and what I know will be a long, sinfully pleasurable night.

CONCUBINE

Portia Da Costa

'm bored. Tell me one of your stories...one of those naughty little sex fantasies you're so good at. Oh, go on, have pity on me, Merry."

"Do you think that's such a good idea, under the circumstances? You know you're supposed to be taking things easy."

"Oh, please, love...I'll take my chances. Give a man a break."

"I would have thought you'd had quite enough of those already."

"Don't worry, I might have broken my ankle, but the rest of me works just fine."

"That's just what I'm afraid of, Rick."

"I'll behave, I promise."

"Oh, very well then. Just because it's you."

"You're a star, love. I love you, you know that, don't you?"

"I should hope so, you sweet-talking devil. Okay, are you sitting comfortably? Then I'll begin..."

* * *

The night was hot and sticky, and as the air pressed down heavily on her skin, Merissa the Fair looked down at the man on the couch before her and tried to will herself into his fitful dreams.

My Lord, I'm here. It's me, Merissa, your concubine.

In a swirl of flimsy silk and satin drapery, she crouched down beside him, letting her fingers glide over the cushion-strewn couch because she dared not yet touch the man himself, or allow herself to caress his beloved skin.

"Alaric," she murmured, touching his hand. He stirred slightly, sighing in his sleep, and Merissa prayed that he was free from pain. Most of it was over now, but there were still some terrible moments.

Could he be feigning sleep? she wondered. He was a brave man and as proud and regal as befitted his long, noble lineage. Did he feel humiliated by his own defenselessness at this time? Ashamed that he couldn't pull her body to his, then crush her beneath him in a fierce act of sex?

But sleep or no sleep, sex or no sex, there was no denying his beauty. For as long as she'd been aware of him—from afar, or closer than close—Merissa had always adored her handsome prince. And she had always been astounded that a man so male could at some times look so exquisite. Granted he had a beard, and a ferocious facial scar from an earlier battle, but his bold masculine features had a purity and finesse that were spine-chillingly ambiguous at times. Merissa loved this magical quality and was completely bewitched by it, but she also loved his virile physique, his athletic skill and strength...and last, but by no means least, his potent, substantial cock.

She couldn't see that now, alas, but she could see almost everything else. To be as comfortable as he could in the intense summer heat, her beloved was naked. Well, almost naked. His body servant—a conscientious soul, ever mindful of his master's dignity—had respectfully covered the princely genitals. A swath of shimmering ocean-blue silk was draped across Alaric's groin. It was roughly the size of a handkerchief, and sheer at that, but apart from a broad white bandage protecting a chest wound, it was the only thing covering his lean, magnificent body. Thinner now, and with numerous freshly healed scars, he still retained in full his power to enflame her senses effortlessly.

And there were new delights to savor. His fair, lustrous hair had gone unbarbered for many months, and it fanned across his pillow now like tangled golden silk; his beard, once so precisely trimmed, looked thicker and wilder and deliciously dangerous, like that of a rogue or a pirate.

There are no two ways about it, Merissa, she told herself, *he's quite perfect.* Slowly, she let her gaze drift downward to that nominal wisp of azure silk—and the mighty treasure she knew it barely concealed.

Even at rest he aroused her. Silky moisture trickled in between her thighs, and her breasts, swinging loose and free beneath her light robe, were aching for the touch of his clever hands.

Do you remember that night before you rode off to war, my love? What we did together and how it felt? Think back, my dearest Lord, and remember our pleasure. Remember it and believe it will happen again.

This sumptuous couch was where it had all begun between them, those many, many months ago. But to her the ancient ritual was just like yesterday.

Two bondswomen had prepared her, bathing her skin and pampering it with soft unguents, brushing her russet hair until it gleamed like a shining river and painting her eyes and lips with delicate color. A couple of days earlier, they'd readied her in other ways too, stroking and petting her innocent sex, accustoming her to sensations new and luscious and to the feel of another's fingers between her legs. Very quickly, she'd been eager and ready, sobbing for relief, her body on fire for the ultimate embrace. And then, while she'd burned, they'd deflowered her with a slender ivory rod. One careful push, one short agonizing shove and the way had been open for the pleasure of her prince.

Smiling for a moment, Merissa despaired of her own naïveté. How could she ever have thought that a man and a dildo could feel the same? When the time came, the differences were as many as the indigo night after the soft golden day.

How wrong could you be, you untutored fool?

Merissa laughed inside at her former self. The dildo had been an object of beauty and carved to *look* real. But it had been hard and cool, quite lifeless. The living prince himself had been just as hard—but also slick and hot and velvety, making her croon with joyous appreciation as he took her.

And she'd crooned again and progressed to all manner of moans and sighs and gasps as he'd thrust inside her, touching a deep, unimagined place she'd never known was there. A place so marvelous and vulnerable that in the end, she'd screamed out his name again and again while her body clasped him.

"Alaric," she whispered now, her sex wet with memories. Memories, and her deep love for this strong man presently laid so low.

And every night since the first night, it had been the same. She'd wake up, her body moist and longing. Then, with the ghost of him inside her, she'd feel a need for him so intense that her fingers would steal between her thighs and she'd stroke her own flesh in his place. Each night since he'd left, she'd parted the folds of her sex and touched what *he'd* touched so sweetly.

And when she could take no more, she'd come in a great chaos of tears and groans and writhing, all the time worshipping his dear face in her mind.

That first night, after she'd fallen asleep in his arms, Merissa hadn't had to resort to such illusions. Just before dawn, her prince had woken her again, and pushed into her so deeply and excitingly she'd almost thought she'd faint. He'd plowed her with an intense and desperate hunger, and she'd welcomed his roughness and reveled in his frantic, almost savage loving. Lying in the darkness, in the thrall of his plunging cock, she could almost believe that somehow he'd be able to stay with her.

And then, in the morning, he'd said, "We'll get married," and frantically kissed her just before he'd swung astride his mighty warhorse. But the marriage of a prince and his concubine was against all court protocol, and as the black months of conflict had passed, that promise had seemed more and more like a trick of her frustrated mind.

But finally, after a wait that had almost destroyed her, she'd heard him make that promise once again.

"We'll get married, Merissa," he'd whispered as they'd carried him past her, victorious but with his body broken and bleeding. His voice had been so faint she could barely hear the words. But his eyes had commanded that she believe.

Oh, yes, they'd be man and wife, she thought, aching for a way to relieve his pain. But when? And when would they ever be lovers again?

No! Stop it! she told herself, looking down at his dear, sleeping face. He'd been gravely injured, but he would recover. And he bore no wounds to his groin or genitalia. It was suffering and exhaustion that had temporarily gelded him, and surely her love could heal that deficiency in time.

Suddenly, she couldn't wait any longer; the time to act was

now. With all the stealth in the world, she whisked away his blue silk covering and sighed at the sight of his beautiful sex.

He was flaccid, as she'd suspected. There was no nocturnal erection to stir the sleepy mass of his flesh. *But don't worry, my Lord*, she told him silently. *I can rouse you, for your pleasure, I know I can.*

And the promise was there. His cock might be soft, nestling against his thick, sand-colored pubic hair, but beneath, his balls looked full and heavy with promise.

"You need relief, my Lord," she whispered, gazing at his body with ravening desire. "And so do I."

In the dreamy silence she imagined him well. His cock rising up. Stiff flesh surging. Overwhelming her. One thrust. No fingers. Straight in. Her fingers tingled and stole blindly downward to where her clit pulsed imperiously. It was that particular time of night again, but just on the point of surrender, she snatched her hand away.

Prince Alaric must come first. He was the center of her world.

So, ignoring her own need, Merissa turned and studied the heavy silver tray that she'd set beside the bed.

On it was an assortment of sensual potions: rare essences dissolved in the purest oils, unguents both soothing and stirring, ointments with which to massage and caress. She'd also brought a bowl of perfumed water and some small, freshly laundered towels, along with a coffer of cooling, finely milled talc. Here was everything she might possibly need to pamper and arouse, and flexing her strong but slender fingers, she could hardly wait to begin.

"Merissa," said the deep, dark voice of her dreams, all of a sudden. Long, unexpectedly dusky eyelashes fluttered like fans, and suddenly her prince was awake.

Merissa knelt, her forehead kissing the carpet. "Forgive me, my Lord. Forgive my foolish impudence."

"Merissa," he said again, quietly, "there's no need for this—" She felt his hand on her shoulder urging her to rise, then heard a ragged gasp.

Up again in a heartbeat, she found him slumped on his pillows, his fine mouth a tight line of pain.

"Is it bad, my Lord?" She nodded at the bandage on his chest.

"No, my love, not too bad. Much better than it was." He seemed about to smile, but just on the point of it, his smooth brow crumpled. "Other things trouble me more." His voice was tense, and Merissa followed the line of his look down past the bandage, across his firm, flat belly...to where his cock lay soft and lifeless.

"I'm no good to you, my sweet Merissa. I can't pleasure you in the way you deserve." He frowned again and his dark eyes went dull, "I love you with all my heart, and yet I'm unable do anything about it. I might never be able."

"But I don't expect to you to make love to me just yet, my Lord. And fucking isn't everything."

The blatant word was exciting. Merissa was shocked to hear it on her own lips, but at the same time she felt strangely empowered. "However, with your permission, sire, there are other activities I'd like to try.... Things that I think might make you feel better." She met his gaze.

After a nervous moment, he smiled, making her feel better, too. "If you'll call me 'Alaric,' my love, you can try whatever you want."

"Very well, my...very well, Alaric." She smiled back at him and then glanced to her tray. "I want you to relax and not move an inch. Lie perfectly still."

Taking up an oil vial, she poured a couple of glistening drops into her palm. She repeated the process with a second vial, then a third, adding more this time. She blended the combination over the entire surface of both her hands and, sniffing her fingers, she smiled at the dizzying result.

Ylang-ylang for sexual stimulus; vanilla for the same; sweet almond oil as a base to nourish the skin.

"Mm...that smells good," Alaric murmured, his voice loose and drowsy. "Do I have to close my eyes to receive this therapy?"

"If you wish, my love." She slanted him her most seductive look. "But you might find it more beneficial if you watch."

"With pleasure, my Merissa."

"I hope so, my...my Alaric."

Merissa settled carefully onto the couch and flexed her fingers again. Bracing her body and her senses, she scrutinized the target area...and what she saw made her heart flutter and leap.

He was responding already, his ruddy shaft thickening and lifting.

I could suck you right now, she thought wildly. *Take you in my mouth and love you. Tease you and taste you until you give up your all in my throat.*

But she curbed her giddy elation and laid her oily fingers carefully on the fronts of his thighs. Her libido was screaming at her to grab him, but to skimp on his promised therapy would be a cheat.

Working with all the precise care and art of a surgeon or sculptress, she kneaded the muscles of his thighs, her lubricated fingers inching only very gradually closer to their goal. Pressure, too, she kept light. It was better to enchant than to attack.

But even though her fingers avoided his cock scrupulously,

her eyes could no longer ignore it. His worries—and hers—had been groundless. She wasn't actually caressing him yet...but she might just as well have been, judging by the vigor of his reaction.

His penis rose like a phoenix unfurling its wings. Working deftly in the hollows of his groin, Merissa could almost hear the mad rush of his blood hurtling toward his sex. Entranced, she saw elegant veining fill up and pulse, his cockhead swelling, stretching, tightening.

She looked up and saw him still watching her. He was observing the frolic of her hands on his skin and the way they made life bloom again in his wounded body. She could feel his will, too, dashing against her like waves: compelling, demanding and ordering like the sovereign he was. *Abandon your task!* it said. *Make an end to this nonsense and touch me now.*

But when he did speak, his voice was soft and earnest: "Caress me, Merissa. Touch me, my darling. I long to feel your lovely hand upon me."

"Patience, my Lord," she commanded, hiding her smile behind her swirling, unbound hair. He hadn't noticed her slip—Prince Alaric had other things than his regal status on his mind.

Working on instinct alone, she lifted his scrotum and slid her fingertips down in beneath it. *Gently, Merissa, gently,* she cautioned. *He's sensitive there...be very, very careful.*

"Yes! Oh, by the very heavens, yes!"

His great shout made a mock of her caution. "Press harder, Merissa. Oh yes, yes, yes!" His beautiful mouth was contorted and working, but this time it wasn't from the pain of his wounds.

Obedient but smiling to herself, Merissa obeyed her lord, trickling her fingers impishly over the whole hot, trembling area of his perineum. With her free hand, she granted yet more mercy...by taking a measured, cradling hold on his rampant cock.

As her fingers pushed below, his flesh leapt above. His shaft waved and throbbed and slithered in her silky, oily grasp, but his erection was as strong and unbending as it had ever been.

He was moaning now. Her name. Endearments. Gibberish. And in the midst of her own growing turmoil, Merissa felt sweet peace dawn.

She had achieved her goal. They had achieved their goal, between them. Her prince was whole at last, and she'd destroyed his doubts and fears. It was only a matter of time before he'd be pleasuring her in return, with his skillful hands, with his body and with his cock.

Mindful of his wounds, she edged across the couch and knelt in the warm space he'd made for her, the space between his widely spread legs.

Almost cross-eyed with awe, she lowered her mouth toward his shaft, drawn to the very tip of it by a twinkling droplet of fluid. It was as if he had a diamond balanced in his love-eye. Merissa was hypnotized. Pointing her tongue, she lapped at the drop greedily, then swallowed it down to absorb the flavors.

Layers of vanilla and almond hovered deliciously in her mouth, but it was mostly Alaric she tasted, beloved and wonderful. Intoxicated, she dove in for more to savor.

"Merissa!"

As she engulfed his shaft, she heard a sob of pleasure, coming to her as if from a great distance. She ignored it.

Nothing could distract her now. No sound or sight could halt the nimble dance of her tongue. He was red hot, slippery and salty, the thin film of oil adding spice to his own sensual fluid. He was an irresistible drug, and in wetness and heat, Merissa sought out every last zone that was responsive and critical, and she delighted in his every yelp and moan as he acknowledged her exploration.

"My Merissa, my Merissa, my Merissa," he chanted, his battle injuries forgotten as his hips rode up and pumped.

And then, as he roared in triumph, Merissa felt her own body quiver. He was coming, filling her mouth with his semen, yet eerily *her* sex was pulsing, too. It seemed impossible, but it was almost as if *she* was coming along with him, whimpering around his cock as her loins turned to a well of cool white flame.

It was almost a miracle, but where had it started? In her mouth, with him, as she sucked...or in her sex, through the unstoppable force of love?

There was no way to decide and no reason to worry her mind over it—that was, if her mind would even work anymore. Releasing her prize from between her lips, all she could do was collapse in a happy, quivering heap between Alaric's outstretched legs.

As tranquility absorbed her, she felt his hand settle gently on her head.

I love you, Alaric, was her last thought before she dozed.

"Is it true then? Can you really come just from sucking my dick?"

"No, of course not. It was a fantasy, you fool!"

"Oh, that's a shame. 'Cos I was thinking of asking you to oblige now you've got me all turned on. Come on, love, give your handsome princey a nice blow job."

"Just because I told you a story about a concubine, it doesn't mean I am one, Rick. I'm still cross with you for doing your ankle in playing football just before our holidays. I'm not sure you really deserve a blow job."

"Aw, Merry, be a sport. You know I'm sorry about the hols. And I will make it up to you. We'll go somewhere fabulous together as soon as I'm all healed up."

"Ah, well, then. Maybe I'll reconsider. But I want a bit of compensation in the short term, too."

"Anything, Princess Merissa, anything... See, his nibs *did* marry his concubine after all!"

"I told you, I'm not your concubine. I'm your missus, and I expect a little *quid pro quo* before I oblige you with oral sex."

"*Quid pro quo?*"

"Yes, payment in kind, matey. I know you've broken your ankle, but there's nothing wrong with your tongue, is there?"

"Ooh, er, not at all, love, not at all. It's in perfect working order."

"Glad to hear that. Now how are we going to organize this? It's going to be a bit awkward, isn't it?"

"We'll manage...we'll manage... Now get your knickers off, Princess Merissa, and we'll work something out somehow."

"Very well, my Lord. Are you lying comfortably? Then let's begin!"

LOVE AND DEMOTION

Logan Belle

If it were any other night, I would be thrilled to be at the book party with him. It's what all of the assistants at the publishing house wanted—even the ones who didn't work for Declan Guinness. We all loved cocktail parties—free food (if you considered cheese cubes and crackers food) and wine, and on our salaries, we needed that more than we wanted to admit. But we especially loved going to parties with Declan. For one thing, we could put our Metrocards away: my boss never took the bus or subway, or even a cab, for that matter—he had a car and driver. Rumor was that he was part of the Irish Brewery family. But money aside (and really, the city was full of rich guys), Declan was beyond gorgeous. And even though I spent all day answering his phone and packing up press kits for his books, when I accompanied him out at night, he was so charming and such a gentleman, it was easy to pretend that I was his date. I know, I know—it was a dangerous fantasy. Declan was my boss, and smart girls just didn't "go there." And I was nothing if not a smart girl.

So when he casually stopped by my desk and said, "It would be great," if I could go to the book party on Park Avenue, I replied, "Sure!" without even thinking about the fact that I had to be in the East Village by ten to do a show. When I tried to get out of going to the party, saying I forgot I had something I had to do, he arched an eyebrow and said mischievously, "Hot date?" Okay, that was inappropriate. But we worked at a book publisher, not a law firm. We were all arty types, and a little humor and banter made everyone's day go faster.

I blushed and babbled, "No, uh, I have to just...be somewhere." To which he replied, "Hmm. Moonlighting?" And that shut me up fast.

"Actually, don't worry about it. I can go," I said. The last thing I wanted was people at work to wonder where I disappeared to three or four nights a week.

"Are you sure? Seriously, Cat, I'm just teasing."

He'd only recently started calling me by my nickname. Before then, it was strictly "Catherine." He'd also recently taken off the platinum wedding band he'd worn for the past five years. I'd only known him for a year of that, but even I'd met the former Mrs. Guinness. She was, not surprisingly, a tall, stunning blonde, her hair a shade so pale and unbrassy that I could only imagine the time and money it required to maintain. Word on the street was that she had traded in Declan for an even richer husband who didn't have a pesky job to take up all his shopping and travel time.

Once the ring came off, I started obsessing about his personal life. Was he dating? What type of woman did he go for? Sometimes I would see his photo in the *New York Magazine* "Intelligencer" pages, and I would scan the party pictures for any hint of who he might be with. And I fantasized about running into him somewhere outside of work, somewhere he would finally see me as someone other than just his assistant.

So there I was, sitting in the middle of a sumptuous living room on the Upper East Side, surrounded by expensive art and skinny women wearing colorful summer tunic dresses and looking like Tory Burch clones. I was sweating despite the air-conditioning because I was wearing a long-sleeved dress to hide my tattoos. I was paranoid about people at work seeing my ink, as if it would somehow reveal my dual life. It was ridiculous, I knew—everyone has tattoos these days. But my Varga girl in a red corset hit a little too close to home.

I pulled my cotton dress open at the neckline and fanned myself with a cocktail napkin. One small table held a pile of the hot-off-the presses cooking memoir (yes, another one) by a *New York Times* editor. She held court in the middle of the room, laughing and drinking in a small crowd that clustered around her. Declan was on the periphery of the group. He looked so beautiful, with his glossy dark hair and Ralph Lauren–model profile, I could barely stand it.

As if sensing my animal stare, he turned to look at me and waved me over with a grin. I was embarrassed at the surge of joy his attention always gave me. Sometimes, a look and a smile from him were enough to make my pussy throb.

Like a hapless puppy, I trotted over to him.

"I want to introduce you to…" I could barely follow what he was saying. Sometimes, when I was near him—especially when we were out of the office—I felt a surge of attraction to him so intense it took all of my willpower not to reach out and touch him.

"I have to leave soon," I told him, hoping he wouldn't ask where I was going. If he did, I was prepared to lie.

"Okay, okay—I know I dragged you here. Thanks for helping out tonight. See you in the morning."

I hated to leave. When I was around Declan, it was like the world was in Technicolor, and when I was away from him, black and white. I had told this to one of the girls at Crushed Velvet, the burlesque club where I performed. She told me that meant I was in love with him.

There was a line outside of the club. It was a sold-out show, and the people standing in the humid July heat were probably waiting for standby seats. Good for them—it would be worth the wait. The theme tonight was "Cinematic Seduction" and all of our performances were tributes to the great movie femme fatales. For me, the choice was a no-brainer: I would be dressed as Lolita and performing to Marilyn Manson's "Heart-Shaped Glasses."

Backstage, in the cramped dressing room, I sat in front of the makeup mirror, naked except for the red Belabumbum thong I would ultimately strip down to in front of the audience. I looked down at the slope of my C-cup breasts and my flat stomach and thought of Declan; it was maddening and ironic that I was the object of desire to crowds night after night, but invisible to the one person I myself desired.

I dusted gold glitter on my eyelids, then attached false eyelashes. I brushed mascara over the eyelashes, then lined the inside and outside of my eye with Sephora black pencil liner until my eyes stood out as dramatically as Lady Gaga's in her "Bad Romance" video.

I squeezed a generous loop of the eyelash glue onto the back of my heart-shaped, red-sequined pasties, and pressed one over each nipple until they stuck. Then I slipped into my short, plaid schoolgirl skirt, and topped it off with an easy-off black corset I'd had specially made by a costumer in Williamsburg. I drew my dark hair into two pigtails, pulled up my thigh-high stockings and stepped into my five-inch platform heels. I finished off the costume with a pair of elbow-length black gloves and, of course, red, heart-shaped glasses. Showtime.

The MC announced me to the audience.

"And now, ladies and gentleman, the fabulous flagellator, your mistress of mischief, Ms. Cat-O'-Nine-Tails!"

Cat-O'-Nine-Tails was my burlesque name, and I almost always included one as a prop in my act. The stage was set for me with a small wooden desk set in the center, covered with hardcover books. By the end of my performance, I would be draped across the desk in only my thong and pasties.

The pulsing, moody strains of "Heart-Shaped Glasses" began, and I stepped out from behind the black curtain. The crowd was quiet except for a few sharp whistles. The music was dramatic, and they were a seasoned enough audience to sense that the tone of my performance would be more erotic than playful. Our shows at the Crushed Velvet ran the gamut, and some of the girls really played their acts for laughs. I admired my friends who could do a tongue-in-cheek number to Katy Perry's "Teenage Dream" or "Diamonds Are a Girl's Best Friend." For some reason, my dances were always more serious. It was part of my sexuality I felt compelled to explore on stage.

I did a few turns and made my way to the front of the stage. By the time the song built to the lyric "Don't break my heart," I shook my ass at the audience and slowly removed one glove. They cheered their approval, and I peeked coquettishly at them over one shoulder while inching off the second glove. I tossed it to the ground, and the crowd whistled and clapped. Stretching my arms out, I arched my back dramatically, and the audience cheered in anticipation of my removing the corset. Instead, I reached down for the cat-o'-nine-tails, and—naughty school-girl that I was—used it to sweep the books off of the desk onto the floor. I stepped one high-heeled foot onto a book and then slowly undid the side clasps of my corset. Facing the audience, I shimmied, cupping my breasts as I eased the corset away.

And then I saw him.

There, in the second row, dead center, was Declan Guinness.

Even though I knew it was him, knew it even before it fully registered with me, I looked back to make sure. And we made eye contact that hit me like an electric shock.

I froze, but only for a second. Quickly recovering, I tossed my corset to the ground, and went on autopilot as I cupped my pasties-covered breasts in my hands and offered them to the roaring crowd.

I'd heard about things like this happening—girls seeing their ex-boyfriends or college friends in the crowd. The key was to just tune them out, and to know that it wasn't you onstage, it was your burlesque persona. Maybe he didn't even recognize me, I foolishly hoped, while another part of me—the part of me that thought of him late at night or when I was putting on my body glitter before shows—hoped that he did.

And it was this part of me that was extremely turned on by knowing he was watching me, finally seeing me as I really was, not as his mousy assistant, breasts and tattoos hidden under button-down shirts from The Gap and shapeless dresses.

As the song built to its crescendo, I pulled off my little schoolgirl skirt and danced over to the desk, where I splayed my body across the hard wooden ledge, one knee bent, toes pointed, arms outstretched, my chest heaving with excitement and exertion. I thought of him watching me and wondered if the audience knew that my expensive thong was suddenly very damp.

* * *

The club had a back exit that let us leave through an alley and avoid the customers. Dressed in my normal clothes, with my makeup removed, I could usually pass right in front of the club and no one noticed me. But tonight I wanted someone to notice me—and he did.

"Cat," he said, stepping out from under the awning of the club.

"What are you doing here?" It felt strange to be that direct—almost accusatory—but the usual dynamic of employer/employee had fallen away the minute my corset hit the floor.

"I'm sorry," he said.

"It's okay...I mean, it's a free country. I just want to know why."

He hesitated for a beat.

"I heard a rumor that you did this. I was curious about it, but I didn't know where or when. And so tonight, when you were in such a hurry to leave the party, I had my driver follow you and text me where to find you."

I had no idea how to respond to this, so I said nothing. And then I remembered,

"It was a sold-out show," I said.

"I hate to break it to you, but your ticket counter accepts bribes."

We stared at each other and I fought the urge to break eye contact first.

And then he reached out and took the duffel bag off of my shoulder.

"Let me carry this for you," he said. And just like that, it was understood that wherever I was going next, he was coming with me.

I walked west, toward my apartment on Bank Street, because

I didn't know where else to go. Declan walked beside me silently. When we reached Greenwich Avenue, I stopped and said, "This is probably a bad idea."

"I know," he agreed, a little too quickly.

"I mean, work and everything," I said lamely, trying to open the door for negotiation.

He stopped walking and we faced each other under the light of a streetlamp. He was still wearing the dark blue pin-striped shirt he'd worn to the party, and I thought of how I had looked at him across the room just a few hours ago, never imagining in my wildest masturbatory fantasy that I'd be standing with him a block from my apartment debating the wisdom of a hookup.

"Yeah, about that." He smiled and ran his hand through his thick hair. It was a move I'd seen countless times in long editorial meetings or when he was on the phone in his office, and I always felt the same urge to follow his motion with my own hand. "Cat, you are so damn distracting to me."

"What? I'm distracting to *you*?"

"Yeah. Can't you tell? I can barely take my eyes off you. It's so unprofessional. And how many times a day do I stop by your desk? I mean, come on—I don't need that much assistance."

I was shocked. How could I be so clueless?

He grinned at me and it was so adorable I wanted to throw myself against him right there on the street.

"Could you tell—I mean, is it obvious that I feel the same way?"

"Yeah," he said.

"It is?" I was mortified. I thought I'd played it so cool.

"Sort of. I never would have said anything if I didn't think it was mutual. I don't want to, you know, sexually harass you."

"You're not," I said.

"Not even just a little?" That grin again.

"Hmm. Maybe a little." And we stood there, smiling at each other like crazy people. Until I couldn't stand it anymore, and I took a step forward and put my arms around him.

I kissed the side of his face, and then our mouths met, and I kissed him hungrily, like it was the last kiss I'd ever have. It was such a relief to feel his arms circle my waist, pulling me closer. I realized how afraid I'd been that this would never happen and that I'd have to live with that.

We separated after a minute, and he said, "Are we really going to do this?"

"Do what?" I said. Because somehow in that moment I still wasn't sure where this was going.

"Fuck," he whispered, his mouth against my ear, lost in my hair. And with that one word, the way he said it, I knew that he was going to be better than any fantasy.

We walked up the five flights to my apartment without talking, without holding hands. But as soon as I closed the front door, he pulled me to him again. I felt him hard through his pants, and I wanted to touch him but something held me back. As much as I wanted to pretend it didn't matter, the work thing was somehow there, making me second-guess my sexual impulses.

He sat on my couch.

"Do you have a roommate?" he said.

"No."

"Okay...then I have a request."

"What?" I asked, guarded.

"Will you dance for me?"

"What do you mean?" Even though I knew.

"Like you did tonight—but here, just for me. It makes it easier for me to see you naked as Cat-O'-Nine-Tails, not as my assistant."

Normally, I would bristle at someone asking me to perform for them. That wasn't something I did on command or to amuse men—ever. But I understood what he was asking: he needed to see me as just a woman.

I put my iPod into the dock and scrolled for the right song. I decided on "My Superman" by Santigold. It was one of the sexiest songs I knew, and as soon as the languid opening beats filled the room, I found it easy to slip into a slow, seductive dance. Without a costume or props, the removal of my clothes felt more like a lap dance than a burlesque striptease, but by the time I got down to my tank top and underwear, all I could think about was how his hands would feel on me and inside of me. As the song drew to a close, I sat on his lap, straddling him in my tank top and underwear. He pulled down one strap, revealing my breast, which he took into his mouth. Something about the fast movement seemed incredibly audacious to me, and very, very hot.

His tongue teased my nipple, and I pressed my already wet pussy against his erection. He pulled off my top and cupped both of my breasts with his hands, brushing his thumbs over my nipples so gently I wouldn't have felt it if it was a part of my body that wasn't so exquisitely sensitive.

"You're perfect," he breathed.

I felt the same way about him.

His fingers traced the Varga girl on my right arm.

"Why do you hide this?" he asked.

When he realized I had no intention of explaining myself to him, he took my breast in his mouth, and a shiver of pleasure shot straight through to my pussy. I leaned down between my legs and fumbled with his belt. He helped me and I swung one leg off of him so I could ease his pants down. His thick cock was straining at his blue cotton boxers, and I immediately grasped him through the opening. His skin felt incredibly warm to my touch, and all I could think about was getting him inside of me.

I tugged his boxers down, and his cock was even more impressive than I'd imagined through his pants. He was big and uncircumcised—my preference, though I rarely encountered it. I slid my hand over the head to pull back the foreskin, and I leaned down to run my tongue around the tip.

He worked his hands into my panties. I was so wet, he easily slid his finger deep inside me. I groaned as he moved it slowly in and out, his thumb toying with my clit. The way he touched me was so perfect, it was as if we were longtime lovers. My body felt like it was vibrating with pleasure, and I couldn't focus on working my mouth on his cock. I was too busy moaning and saying things like, "Oh, god," and other mindless exclamations I said when someone got me to that place where I couldn't think, only feel. I was close to coming, but I wasn't ready; I wanted it to be on that gorgeous cock of his. This wasn't the office, after all, and in the bedroom, I liked to do things my way.

I pulled his hand away, and he looked quizzical at first, but when I straddled him he quickly got with the program. He held my ass as I lowered myself onto his cock, the length of it wet from my mouth. Our eyes met as he filled me, and I felt a tug of something that was much more than lust. Was my friend at Crushed Velvet right? Was I in love with him?

We rocked together gently at first, and then he adjusted himself and held my hips, thrusting hard into me. His mouth moved hungrily from my breasts to my neck, and then we were kissing hard and fast, and then he took my lower lip gently between his teeth and it gave me a chill. I sat up so I could look at him, my spine almost straight, my hair fanning out against my back. He reached up and cupped my breasts, his big blue eyes sweeping from my face down my body and back up again.

"You're so beautiful," he whispered.

"You are," I said. He closed his eyes, and I bent down to kiss his brow. He swept one hand through my hair, his cock pushing even deeper. In that instant, I came, my pussy shuddering against him in waves that seemed like they would never stop. And then he made a guttural, animalistic sound and I could feel an extra vibration of his cock that signaled he was going to come. I leaned down, my breasts against his chest, and he circled one arm around my waist to hold me to him, his other hand firm on my ass. He pushed into me so hard and fast it was like I was riding an animal.

"My god," I said, and I came again.

"I feel you," he breathed, his mouth wet against my neck. I was almost embarrassed that I kept coming, and even when his body quieted to a stop, my pussy clenched against him greedily, as if trying to resuscitate a heart.

He pulled me next to him, my head resting on his outstretched arm. We breathed against each other quietly for a minute or two, staring up at the ceiling.

"Well," he said finally. "This presents a problem."

"No one at the office has to know," I said.

"I think they'll find out eventually."

"Eventually? In a few days it will be like this never happened," I said.

"I'm hoping that in a few days, this will be happening again," he said. "And then again a few days after that. With some dinners and movies in between, I think. If that's okay with you."

I propped myself up on one elbow and looked at him. His cheeks were flushed, a beautiful contrast to his dark hair that made his eyes an even brighter blue. I was too awed by him to be sure of what he was saying.

"I thought this was a one-night thing. I mean, we work together. You're my boss."

"I don't have to be," he grinned.

"Unlike you, I actually need that lame paycheck."

"I'll help you find another one."

Now I sat straight up, pulling the sheets around my bare breasts.

"You're not serious."

He sat up, smiling, and took my face in his hands. He kissed me gently on the lips.

"I don't think dating my assistant is a very wise idea. What would you suggest?"

I stared at him, and soon my smile matched his.

"So, what are you saying?" I asked, my heart beating hard. I felt like I was standing on the edge of cliff.

He took my hand.

"You're fired," he said.

I smiled and, taking a leap off that cliff, climbed right back on top of my former boss.

MEPHISTO WALTZ

Justine Elyot

They say his fingers have been insured for a million dollars per hand. Watching them fly over the keys with that preternatural sureness of touch, I can believe it, too. He spans an octave and a half effortlessly, never having to stretch or strain like me, with my stupid stunted claws. Perhaps that's his secret. But I think there's more to it than that.

"He really used to teach you?" Sophie's whisper is tense with awe. "Oh, my god. How did you not jump his bones at the piano stool?"

"Sophie, I was twelve years old."

"Lily, he is the sexiest man on the planet."

"Shh, I want to listen to the music."

Liszt's first Mephisto Waltz has become his signature tune, astonishingly difficult to play at all, let alone play well, as my many hours spent in futile battle with it can testify. He storms through the thunder-and-lightning opening, though, tossing his hair while his hands blur into the white keys, his eyes manic with intensity. He is no less flamboyant now than he was as a student at the Conservatoire. Now he is famous for his jewel-colored silk waistcoats and cravats rather than the skinny jeans and psychedelic shirts he favored in his penniless teaching days. I can see why Sophie is sitting there open-mouthed, just like his legion of female fans who follow him from tour date to tour date, crowding him in a hysterical gaggle at the stage doors every night. Yes, he is attractive, but there is no need to actually drool, surely.

Moving on from the attack on the waltz proper, he tackles the quieter passages, bending his long spine so that he almost hugs the keyboard, his nose inches from the ivory, ready to kiss the notes into the air. This section of the piece could so easily descend into cloying sentimentality, but there is something about his well-harnessed power that prevents that while retaining the emotional spirit of the music. It is quite a trick. It is something I have never learned.

Maybe today, though; maybe today is the day I become a real musician.

I am hopeful as he takes the final bars of the waltz and alternately charms and brutalizes them into submission. The notes obey him. He will teach me how to make the notes obey me.

A storm of rapturous applause—standing ovation, screams, fainting, the full adoring works—greets his final flourish. He holds his hand above the keyboard in midair for a few seconds, and we all watch it slowly descend before he leaps to his feet and performs a series of energetic bows, accepting the plaudits as his natural due.

Leonid Gorodetsky, superstar.

He exits stage left and the crowds begin to drift off, buzzing excitedly as I struggle past in their slipstream. Sophie and I head the opposite way, up to the stage and across to the wings.

A frowning youth with a clipboard halts me at the curtain.

"I'm Lily Arliss," I tell him. "I won the competition. I'm here for my master class with Mr. Gorodetsky."

"Right, right," he says, shuffling pages. "Lily Arliss. Right. Yeah. Um, hold on, I'll get someone to show you to the green room."

While he scampers off, I turn to Sophie.

"Wish me luck."

"Wish you luck! You've already had all the luck! You have one whole afternoon of that sex god's undivided attention. I'm so jealous I might have to die."

"Oh, don't do that."

"Swap with me?" she asks slyly.

"I don't think so."

"Ah, well. Be good. Give me a ring when it's over."

She steps back off the stage and joins the residue of the lunchtime concert throng, leaving me alone with what I'm ridiculously thinking of as my destiny.

The green room is tatty with peeling paint and I spend an age reading ancient playbills over and over until I am able to recite the cast of the 1996 season of Alan Ayckbourn comedies from memory. My promise to myself not to be nervous lies in fragments. I feel sick with tension, my head compressed in a tight rubber band.

It's just your old piano teacher, Lily.

My stomach jolts at the sound of his voice in the corridor outside, that low, clear, Russian accent that used to tell me to "Make the notes siiing, Lily." Instantly, I am twelve again, kicking my sensible shoes against the piano stool, driving myself to play the same phrase over and over again until I have his approval.

"Okay," he is saying to some invisible minion. "I know. But if the flight leaves at ten I still have time for...okay. I'll see you then."

He is in the doorway, jacket and waistcoat off, cravat loosened, the sleeves of the white dress shirt rolled up to the elbow. His forearms rest against the frame and his hair falls over one eye as he sizes me up and squints, making an effort to place me, I suppose. My insubordinate heart refuses to slow down. He is so much taller than I remember and somehow fuller and more colorful. In my memory I had a line drawing of a long, thin thing with a big nose and hair that needed cutting. In reality, I have before me simply the most attractive man I have ever seen.

"Hello," he says uncertainly, then suddenly he springs into action, stepping through the door and pointing one long, excitable finger at me. "Lily! Lily Bancroft! You have changed your name. You are married?"

"No. Deed poll. Didn't want my father's name anymore."

He blinks, but chooses not to ask the loaded question. I stand and smile at him, the nerves gone, replaced by simple and genuine joy at seeing him again. It's not often I have a simple feeling, and I try to make the moment last, reaching out for one of those precious hands, which he graciously places in mine.

Gorodetsky's hand. I am holding his legendary hand. Those women outside by the rubbish bins would kill to be in my position. It's a very nice hand, too, warm and smooth, nothing limp or clammy about his grip. It's the hand I remember from my childhood. The magic hand, the hand that turns notes and chords into sensual experience and fills the critics' heads with hyperbole. I feel as if I ought to light up, or crackle, or something. Actually, I'm not far off crackling.

"You are all grown up and yet you look exactly the same," he remarks. "That dark, closed, driven girl. I never had a more promising pupil, but I used to pray every night that you might just lighten up a little bit."

"Really?" I am taken aback. I was not expecting psychoanalysis within our first few minutes of reunion, and I feel rather stung. Perhaps I would cry, if it was something I ever did.

"Well, perhaps I didn't pray exactly. Hope."

"I'm sorry your hopes were dashed," I say tightly, tugging my hand from his. "For what it's worth, you've changed a great deal. You used to be kind."

"Lily! I didn't mean to hurt you. I'm sorry. Can we go to the rehearsal room now? I'm looking forward to hearing you play again, twelve years later. I want to know what you've learned."

He puts a hand on my shoulder, steering me gently to the door, and I let him lead me, feeling a little ashamed of my outburst. How temperamental. I shudder a little and vow to appease any offense I may have caused him.

"It didn't surprise me that you turned out to be such a success," I tell him. "I knew you were a genius, even then."

"Thank you." His smile is glorious, transforming a face that could be called dour or severe in repose. "It still surprises me sometimes. It's a mad life. You know, occasionally, I want to go back to the Conservatoire days of freedom."

"And penury."

"Well, yes." He laughs. "But penury can be fun, if you have your passions."

We are at the rehearsal room, cavernous and dusty and smelling of the school gymnasium.

He unstacks two iron-framed chairs and sits on one, gesturing me to face him on the other. His legs are elegantly crossed and he looks relaxed. How does that feel, I wonder? I take my place opposite, feeling that I have been called for an interview.

"I need you to tell me what you want from this master class."

"I want to play like you."

"Technically or...?"

"Oh no, not technically. I can play the notes. I have no problems with the most complicated cadenzas. I want that thing that you put into the notes. I don't have that. I have to have it, and I don't think anyone else can show me how to do it."

He looks up at the ceiling and sighs, as if faced with a conundrum.

"What are your passions, Lily?"

I want to laugh hysterically at the idea of the godlike Gorodetsky asking me, in a tone that could be interpreted as seductive, about my passions. *Of course he doesn't want to seduce me. Of course it's just that foreign thing of speaking your mind and coming straight to the point. He is asking me about my interests, that's all.*

I titter palely. "Well...music, of course."

"And?"

I don't know where to look.

"I quite like doing crosswords."

This is the wrong answer, I gather. He stares at me as if I have told him I enjoy eating the brains of decapitated kittens, then he says, "I see," followed by another horrible silence.

He waves an imperious arm in the direction of the piano.

"Play for me," he says.

"What...shall I play?"

"What do you want to play?"

"I want to play the first Mephisto Waltz."

"Oh, really?" His eyebrows disappear skyward. "I have competition, do I? Go on then."

I sit at the stool, going through my father's old mantra: spine straight, shoulders back, arms relaxed, wrists loose. I put my feet on the pedals and lift the lid. I depress the middle C, just to make sure the instrument is in tune. It is. Right. Deep breath. And play.

The notes tumble out and I put them in their places. I change the tempo and the volume when required. A couple of quavers get away, but I manage to put the error right and carry on, breathing shallowly now, wrestling with the music, convinced it will fall into ruin if I don't keep it in rigorous order.

I see him get up and walk toward me and around the piano. He is stroking his chin, looking worried, lost in thought. I make it to about three minutes before he puts up a hand and says, "Stop, stop, stop!"

I take my fingers off the keys immediately. "That bad?" I ask.

"It's not bad," he says, leaning over my shoulder. "Technically it's good. Excellent, even."

"But?"

"Have you ever really listened to this piece? Do you know what it is about?"

"Yes, I do! It's about Mephistopheles playing wild music on the violin while Faust dances with a beautiful villager."

"Oh, Lily, Lily. Mephistopheles's playing is supposed to be 'incredibly seductive and intoxicating.' Faust and his partner 'waltz in mad abandon.' You play this piece almost faultlessly, but I am not seduced. I am not intoxicated. I do not have any sense of mad abandon at all. Where *is* your passion, Lily? Where is it hiding?"

I think I understand this crying business after all. My voice is a little husky when I answer him. "I do have passion," I insist. "My passion is all given to learning to play better. Learning to be a musician."

"Passion is not learnt. It is felt. Take my hand."

I have a stubborn desire to ignore him, but I give him my grudging fingers and he pulls me to my feet, holding me then by my upper arms, tightly, as if the closer his grip the more likely it is that I will understand him.

"When you play the piano," he says, feeling for the words. "You are not together. The piano is like your enemy."

My eyes fly wide. He is right. I had never thought of it like this, but he is absolutely right. It has always been something to be conquered.

"What...should it be?"

"Your lover, Lily. Your partner. You feed it your love and it responds to that. Like a kiss."

I can't say the words that come into my head; I can't say them to him. He will laugh at me. He says them for me, leaning low from his great height.

"You have kissed, haven't you?"

He looks so *worried* for me that I want to reach up and stroke his cheek. How inappropriate. I delete that thought with a harsh laugh.

"None of your business."

He jerks back, wounded. "None of my business? It is my business to show you how to play the piano. I don't think you can do it until—"

"What rot!" I exclaim, terrified and yet wildly exhilarated by the unspoken suggestion. "Plenty of virtuosi have been..."

"Virgins? Maybe. But I don't think that will work for you. Those people still knew how to release their passion. You don't."

"I don't think it's that important, that's all."

"Why not? You are afraid. Who taught you after me?"

"My father."

"Ah, okay. I see."

"He couldn't afford to hire another tutor."

"His methods were different, I'm sure."

"Yes, they were." We fall silent. I think about my father's methods. I think about my adolescence, metaphorically chained to the piano stool, the hours of scales, the absence of company.

"Well, I can't use those methods," says Leonid eventually. "Perhaps we should end the class."

"No," I say, suddenly and forcefully. "No. I want what you've got and I'll do anything to have it."

His grip on my arms had relaxed but it tightens again at that.

"Look at me, Lily," he says, drawing my eyes magnetically up to his. The connection almost overwhelms me, a sideways shake of the earth. *He cares about me.* "I want to help you more than I can say," he says softly. "I think I could help you. But you would have to trust me."

"Okay," I whisper. "So...shall I go back to the piano?"

I seem to be trembling. When he releases one arm to put a finger on my lip, it turns to a rather embarrassing violent palsy. He says nothing, but shakes his head and waits. What is he waiting for? His hand cups my face, and it is so big and fits so well, I have to nuzzle into it. I have never felt anything on this scale. It is unquantifiable, alien to me. Fear makes me want to speak words of repudiation, but none will come; my brain is too busy processing this enormity of physical reaction.

"Show me," he murmurs, "passion."

I am on tiptoes, leaning into him, when an ugly thought pierces the resolve.

"Do you do this to all your pupils?"

"No!" he shouts, pushing me away. "If that is what you think, then..."

"I don't think anything!" I shout back. "I'm scared, Leonid, scared to death of you. Of me. Of what you do to me."

He turns away for a moment, clutching his forehead, then wheels back, swooping down to me, hands on my wrists again.

"Take the fear," he says. "And leave. Or else, turn it into something else. Turn it into—"

With a gasp of pure frustration, his lips are on mine, his million-dollar fingers in my hair, messing it up. I had been so careful with the clips and combs and spray earlier, but it doesn't matter anymore.

My third kiss, and it is nothing like the others. No alcohol on the breath, no drooling, no limp lips. This is how it is meant to be. I have been wrong all these years to be disappointed in kissing—it is the *kissers* who have let me down. Leonid has lips that sing, just like his fingers, and into me he pours all that fire and fury that echoes around the concert halls of the world. Not even a token spark of resistance can be mustered on my side; instead I yield, totally and instantaneously, melting into him, wanting to be him, and have him, and hold him in a permanent kiss.

Oh, that's his tongue! I have never gone so far before, and rather than finding it disgusting, I just want more, deeper, farther, harder. It feels like walls crumbling, like old orders dying, it feels like *music*. And now I can see how the music can be mine. Now I see it.

In my euphoria, I am not sure whether to break the kiss or continue it, but he leaves me no choice, his hand tight at the back of my head, locking me into the embrace. Once my lips are stinging and my face is damp and the tears have come, he lets me out, but his face is still so close, nose to nose, his eyes looking behind mine, into my soul.

"You have it," he says. "You have so much of it."

"But it's for you," I whisper to him in despair. "You, not the piano."

"Why not for both?"

"I don't want to play now. I just want you to kiss me again."

"Lily, I can turn this class into something more. If you want."

"Something more?"

"Your talent," he says, his fingers pressing into the soft flesh of my neck. "It needs to be nurtured. I want to do that."

"You want to be my teacher again?" The disappointment is sickening.

"I want to teach you more than piano." The elation is frightening. "I want to show you what you can be, and what you can have, because you have no idea, do you?"

"No," I confess, my voice a tiny waver.

"So, if I kiss you again, do you understand that it might lead somewhere?"

Somewhere? Sex! The big bugbear of my life. The monster in my closet.

"Leonid, I've never..."

"I know." He kisses the tip of my nose. "Do you want to?"

"Only with you. Because I trust you. I trust you not to hurt me."

"Thank you. That must take a lot of courage. The trust, I mean."

I rub my nose into his. I love his nose, so solid, something to push against.

"This is the weirdest day of my life," I tell him.

"I hope it will become the best," he says. "Come."

He leads me over to the piano stool and sits down on it, his back to the keyboard, before pulling me down on to his lap.

"Now," he says, before resuming his ravishing of my lips and face, "I am giving you a lesson in harmony. Take note, Lily."

I am entangled in his arms and legs; they creep around me like elegant, muscular vines, imprisoning me in a pleasure cell. My lips don't care that they are sore because they drink him down, let him inside, give him the run of my intimate oral space. The brilliant hands begin to search and seek their targets, first my neck, which they stroke and press until I am jelly, then one moves around to undo the top button of my blouse, reading the messages of my skin through its sensitive fingertips. They know how to interpret the changes in heat just as well as they interpret a passage of Beethoven. A million dollars is not enough. These are the best fingers in the world; they should be memorialized in the grandest museums; he should keep them in velvet-lined boxes and lock them away in a safe.

"Harmony," he murmurs in a rare moment of lip freedom, and he moves my hands from where they are anchored on his shoulders, making it clear that he wants me to touch him, too.

This is the worrying part, for I do not feel that I know how to touch, and I fret that my clumsiness will deter him from this now-urgently-needed lesson.

"Put them wherever you like," he advises me, "but don't be afraid."

The kiss is back, and I make a bold move inside his loose shirt collar, enjoying the protrusion of bone and the flatness of chest inside there. Is there hair? Yes, but just a little. Oh, and a nipple. Of course I knew men have nipples. I'm not *that* repressed. All the same it makes me want to giggle to actually feel its rubbery flex beneath my finger. He almost bites my mouth off when I flick at it, and then he pulls my blouse out from the waistband of my skirt and presses hot palms against my back, my stomach, creeping upward in an inevitable path.

I moan into his throat as the cotton cups of my ever-sensible bra are wrenched down over my nipples. It is almost painful; they are as hard and full of blood as they'll ever be, and oh, how he knows how to play them. I begin to squirm in his lap at the exquisite torment of it. Every brush, every tweak, every flip of the thumb sends a flame-colored streak of pleasure straight down to my crotch. My knickers are getting wet, uncomfortably so; the combined devilry of his tongue and his fingers are making me want to howl with lust. Lust! This is lust! A word I never thought would enter my vocabulary.

In the tangle of all this, I have managed to unbutton his shirt and now his taut abdomen is open and ready for me to rub myself against. His arms are so strong, I can see now how he has the stamina for those recitals of entire sonata cycles. I doubt I'll ever have that kind of power, but I can have the finesse, I can have the emotion, it is all within my reach—if only I can undo that belt buckle.

We reach for the waistbands at the same time and his back shifts against the keyboard, making it growl a low discord.

"Stand up," he mutters, and he deals with my zipper swiftly, letting the skirt flounce to the floor before pulling me back, in my underwear with my blouse hanging open, to further devour me. I wrestle the belt from its loops and drop it with a clink. Now I am getting to the heart of the action. Now I am close to that strange lump that has been digging into my buttocks for the last ten minutes.

But he is so busy burrowing his way inside my knickers that I am distracted from my mission and I have to stretch back against him and lie there, open-mouthed, while his hand sneaks smoothly over my mons and parts the lips beyond.

My breath loses its rhythm. I feel the remnants of shame, as if I ought to be slamming my legs shut and slapping his face. But how do the good girls do that, when this feels so good? How do they resist? I am lost to the good-girl brigade now, pushing myself down on his magical digits, begging wordlessly for more.

"Has a man ever touched you here?" His breath is hot and ragged in my ear.

"No." I spread my legs wider, on either side of his knees,

wanting to know how this works, how it will end.

"I think you must like it. You're very wet."

"That means I like it?"

"Yes. You can't deny it, Lily."

I can't deny it. Why would I? I am outside myself now, outside my walls, running free. I am a woman, everywoman, enjoying sex, enjoying getting fingered by a man. A man she loves.

His words in my ear trickle down through the center of my body to my groin, where they explode in a wondrous whirlwind of abandonment. I am all sensations, all sensuality, all *passion*. He kisses me as I come, taking my cries inside him as if they are manna he has teased from me and must eat to survive.

I suffer and settle and subside into his arms. I have given him something. I hope he will not abuse it. I knew that sex was scary, I suppose, but now I am hard up against the dread and, while it is severe, it is not as bad as I had assumed. It is worth it. I would do it again.

"Now," he whispers into my ear, "I want you to do that for me. I want you to try and get the response you want from me. Use your fingers, use your lips, use your brain, use your senses. I am your instrument. Play me."

Here is an exercise I never thought I would be given. It is the most daunting and the most exciting challenge of my life—none of the competitions I have entered come close to this. I give the side of his neck a tentative kiss; I feel him stiffen and I deepen it. So far so good. But what to do with my hands? Where best to deploy them?

I make discoveries; his nipples jump when I touch them and he likes to be bitten and sucked on the flesh around his neck and shoulder. I take courage from these modest successes to move down to his waistband. I unbuckle the belt and remove it from the loops, but now I am having severe misgivings. *If I should fail...?* With trembling fingers, I undo his trousers, letting the disembodied voice of Lady Macbeth urge me onward and downward. *But screw your courage to the sticking point...*

My sticking point springs upward out of its fabric confinement, and here I am, confronted with the male member for the very first time. Not just any male member either—the tall, vigorous male member of Leonid Gorodetsky. The penis of the pianist. But I have to stop making myself giggle. I have to stop all this childish self-consciousness. I have to *play* him.

My fingers brush against it, hardly knowing what to expect. They get softness, warmth, sleekness backed by steel. I had thought, for some reason, it would bend. It does not, and he yelps when I establish this fact.

"Sorry."

"It's okay. Go ahead. Touch. Feel. Do what you want. Try not to hurt me."

I look for ways to overwhelm him; I try them out with clenched fist and open palm, with sealed lips and slick tongue. I tweak and twiddle, stroke and pump, and I use the way he responds as my guide. More of this, less of that, lots of the other, combining to force those happy, helpless sighs from him, until I find the right combination. One hand on his balls, one wrapped around the base of his shaft, my mouth tackling the rest, building up rhythm, combining in a three-part harmony. He feels limp now, and yet tense at the same time; helpless, but keeping that awesome power of his in reserve. I sense the crescendo, I am heading for the fortissimo, but I will take it as it comes, play it the way it should be played.

His flavor is addictive, but the way he explodes into my mouth is more so, filling me with a taste I have never experienced. He roars into climax and no standing ovation could ever be sweeter. The bouquets fall around me and I glow with the satisfaction of a piece well interpreted. My lover is mine, I have made him mine. I can do the same with the music now.

"What will you do? Must you stay here?" he asks me, holding me close as we lie in languid discomfort on the top of the grand piano after I have played—stunningly—the first Mephisto Waltz again.

"Must I?" I muse. "No, I suppose not. What is keeping me here really? My father."

"You owe him nothing," says Leonid urgently. "You owe him less than nothing. Years in the dark, Lily. That is all he has given you. Come with me. Come to Budapest. Come to Rome. Come to Moscow."

I try to sit up but he pulls me back down. "Leonid? You aren't serious?"

"I want to get you out of this rainy city, away from that man, away from your past. I want you to be free. You know what they say about setting free the one you love."

"Isn't that what people say to rationalize dumping some-body?" I snark, but then the vista opens up before me and I feel that jumping-from-a-plane exhilaration. "Do you think you could bear to have me tagging along on your endless world tour?"

"I don't think I could bear it if you didn't."

I nod him a speechless yes. The music is my life now. The first bar is written. Now for the symphony.

THEN

Emerald

Would you grab the gift on the table, please?" I called to Chris as I shrugged into a light jacket and waited for him by the door.

Chris appeared in the foyer a few seconds later, studying the package in his hand. The sparkling wrapping paper was almost blinding as it reflected the setting sun streaming through the window. "It's very...bright," he said, grabbing his own jacket.

"Sarah loves bright things," I reminded him, taking the box from him. I tucked the envelope I was holding under the royal-blue ribbon and smiled at the glittering package. "Ready?"

Though the party had only started a half hour before, there were a couple dozen people already filling Sarah and Shawn's house when Chris and I squeezed through the door fifteen minutes later. I set Sarah's present on a table beside the basket filled with various colored envelopes.

"Valerie!" Sarah called my name as she appeared in the crowd and wove through it to greet us.

"Happy birthday," I said, as I enveloped her in a warm hug. "Sorry we're a little late." I stepped back and turned to Shawn, who had come up beside her. As he hugged me delicately, careful not to spill the glass of wine in his hand, I caught sight of a tall figure with his back to me, standing near the kitchen. As I watched, the figure turned, and the suspicion fueling the low heat forming inside me was confirmed.

It was Hayden.

For a moment, my stomach disappeared as the same jolt of arousal sizzled through me that had every time I had laid eyes on Hayden. I hadn't seen him for a few months—not since the wedding, where I had been Sarah's maid of honor and Hayden was Shawn's best man. I had first met him at their engagement party last year, one that Chris had been unable to attend. My attraction to him had been immediate, intense—and mutual. Looking at him now, I remembered back to that uncomfortable feeling of instability, the guilt of knowing I was intensely attracted to Hayden juxtaposed with the understanding that I had no desire to leave my relationship with Chris.

I caught my breath as Hayden spotted me. Though much had transpired since that time, my physical attraction to him seemed to not have abated at all. I smiled as he approached, stepping forward to embrace him as we exchanged greetings. Though our hug was casual, the shiver from the pit of my stomach to my pussy as he touched me was both familiar and as intense as ever.

I glanced at Chris as I let go. Chris knew about my attraction to Hayden. I lowered my eyes as I remembered the understanding and tenderness with which he had received my monologue when I relayed the whole story. For the first several weeks after meeting—and feeling so intensely attracted to—Hayden, I had found the situation such a conundrum that I'd kept how I was feeling a secret. Then, a few months before the wedding had taken place, I told Chris of my intense infatuation with Hayden and all I'd been experiencing around it.

The revelation had invited an opening between us—as well as within me—as we had found that there was much more going on than just an infatuation with someone else. Chris and I emerged from the conversation that day, one of the most challenging and exhaustive of our three-year relationship, with more awareness about ourselves, each other and the relationship between us. After letting Chris know what was going on, the confusion and consternation I had experienced around my fixation with Hayden had almost entirely abated, and for the most part Hayden had retreated to a fond memory for me, albeit one infused with undeniable arousal on the occasions I indulged in entertaining it.

Thus I supposed the basic attraction I still felt toward Hayden wasn't surprising. I remembered well how I had felt at the wedding; knowing the solidity of affection and dedication I felt for Chris didn't eliminate the feeling of intense attraction to someone else—in this case, Hayden.

I placed my hand on Chris's arm as I backed up. I had introduced the two of them at the wedding, and while I had felt slightly awkward at the time, the brief interaction had seemed cordial. I cleared my throat and reintroduced them, my cheeks—and my pussy—flaming. Hayden smiled and Chris nodded as the two of them shook hands.

Shawn called Hayden away then. I did my best to catch my breath as I avoided speaking by heading to the food table. I noticed the arousal roiling in the pit of my stomach wasn't so tied up this time with the feelings of guilt and confusion I had experienced when I'd first met Hayden. It was now simply there, a base attraction that I felt some degree of relief knowing Chris was aware of.

Of course, he may not have been aware right then that my panties had grown wet when Hayden touched me. I almost jumped when he said, "You look a little flushed."

I looked up to find Chris studying me closely. I couldn't tell if his tone held a note of awareness or not. His face was impassive as he continued, "Would you like me to get you a drink?"

I nodded and thanked him as I turned and grabbed an hors d'oeuvre. Before he could return, Sarah enlisted my help in the kitchen, and I followed her dutifully, taking a deep breath as I tried to relax.

I refilled a tray of dark chocolate bonbons, only subconsciously scanning the kitchen for a glimpse of Hayden. Placing a mint leaf in the center of the tray, I carried it out to the living room and repositioned it on the food table, then looked around the room for Chris.

I caught sight of him near the patio and made a move to join him before I stopped short. My stomach jumped. He was talking to Hayden.

Nervousness pressed in around me. There wouldn't be a scene, would there?

It took only a few seconds of observation, however, to see that there was no animosity in the interaction; on the contrary, it seemed, as I continued to observe them. The interaction didn't appear casual, but there was no sign of heatedness either. Even from across the room, I could see that neither man's body language displayed indications of hostility or feeling threatened. Hayden's gray eyes were serious, and he nodded a couple times as I watched. Chris clasped Hayden's shoulder as he turned away in a manner that looked more meaningful to me than a friendly gesture.

I had no idea what they'd said to each other, but there was something in the interaction I couldn't place, something that seemed unexpected somehow. I turned and headed back to the kitchen, unable to explain the stab of poignancy that slid through me.

A half hour later, I stood with Shawn outside on the patio.

"You may not know this, but Hayden was cheated on once," he said in a low voice, glancing over my shoulder before he continued. "It hurt him a lot. Obviously that didn't happen with you two, but he told me once that when it occurred to him how close he'd come to being on the other side of that scenario, he'd always wanted to apologize to Chris."

I hadn't known. Shawn added, "He knows Chris already knew about the situation, of course. He wouldn't have said anything if he didn't know you two had already talked about it."

It occurred to me then what I had seen in their conversation that I hadn't placed: vulnerability. It wasn't obvious or prominent, but it had been there. The poignancy I felt when I'd witnessed the conversation returned more strongly, and my eyes dropped as I imagined what it had taken for Hayden to approach Chris and the graciousness Chris had appeared to exhibit in accepting it.

Chris didn't mention the conversation with Hayden during the rest of the party or on the way home. I wondered if he knew I was aware of it.

When we got inside, he said as he shrugged out of his jacket, "Shawn told me you noticed Hayden and me talking tonight."

I turned to him. "I did, yes."

Chris smiled. "He said he'd mentioned to you what it might have been about. He was right. Hayden was very polite. It seemed pretty cool of him to seek me out like that."

"I'm glad," I said, sincerely.

The topic dropped. I felt a combination of gratitude and wistfulness wash over me as we headed up the stairs. Though my attraction to Hayden was still strong, the relief I felt at its being out in the open was immense, and the appreciation I felt toward Chris for not finding it threatening was almost fierce.

I reached for him as we entered the bedroom and wrapped my arms around his waist from behind, squeezing as I pressed my cheek against the smooth fabric of his shirt. He chuckled and lifted my hand to kiss it.

"I love you," I said, my voice muffled against his back.

"I love you, too," he said, unwinding himself and turning around so he could kiss me on the mouth.

After a few minutes I broke away with a smile and headed for the closet, unzipping my dress as I walked. I opened the closet door and almost dropped my dress when Chris said, "So you're interested in Hayden sexually?"

I froze. That was a trick question if there ever was one. Especially since Chris already knew the answer.

"I—well, yes," I answered finally. "I think you were aware of that."

Chris nodded. "I was just seeing if it was still the case."

I stared at him. His tone was neutral, and I had no idea what his motivation would be for pursuing such a discovery.

"Might I ask why?"

Chris turned to me. His blue gaze was still unreadable, but I felt the undercurrent of lust in it that instantly ignited my own. He didn't say anything for a moment, just stared at me like that, almost as though he were wrestling with something inside himself.

"Maybe it's something I might like to watch."

My jaw dropped. It was a suggestion I would never have expected Chris to make.

Of course, one of the things I had experienced as so frustrating about my infatuation with Hayden was that to me, it had never felt like that feeling and my relationship with Chris were even connected—I didn't actually sense a threat to how I felt about Chris in how I felt about and what I wanted to do with Hayden. But convention—and, nonetheless, agreement with Chris—said otherwise, and one of the displeasures of the situation had been wrestling with an attraction to Hayden that seemed so strong it felt like it would take me over, thus realistically threatening a relationship with a man I loved despite how arbitrary and unfair that threat seemed to me.

Still, I had never seen any indication from Chris that he had felt anything similar.

"Watch?" I scarcely dared to breathe as I sought confirmation of what he was saying.

"Watch you fuck him. Would you like that?" Chris crossed the room in three full strides, stopping inches from my body as his eyes, ferocious in their lust-filled state, bored into mine.

I looked at him dizzily, almost faint from both the shock and the arousal the suggestion had evoked.

Chris moved a tiny bit closer until he was almost touching me, until I could feel the heat from his body against my vulnerable, naked skin. "Would you?" The demand was calm; a solid, even cover above the simmering desire I sensed beneath it. My fingers reached out and brushed Chris's cock, fully hard now beneath his trousers as he held my gaze. I felt my heart pounding, my breath coming in hot, ragged gasps as I looked up at him.

"Yes."

I expected to feel nervous, anticipated the adrenaline as I stood in Hayden's bedroom. But as my eyes locked with his as he stood near the foot of his bed, all I felt coursing through me was the unadulterated desire I had felt every time I'd looked at Hayden. My body shuddered as I took a deep breath.

I'd asked Chris the night before what he wanted from this. He'd looked thoughtful. "I want to watch you get what you want," he'd finally answered. "That's what I want."

Chris sat now in the chair to my left, facing the king-sized bed. I looked over at him. His expectant gaze was dark with lust, accelerating my own as I turned back to Hayden. Suddenly I felt shy, like the star of the show, the sole one the audience (in this case, the audience of two) was here to see.

Then Hayden stepped forward, and the spell in me broke. I met him without pause, closing the distance between us the way I'd wanted to since I'd first laid eyes on him. The air in the room went from anticipatory holding pattern to oxygen in the fire the moment we touched each other, the scene shifting from placid to burning as Hayden's hands found my shoulders, my hair, my neck, my breasts as he kissed me. I forgot everything but the touch I had fantasized about so many times as it trailed sparks now over my physical body. My clothes dropped away as I closed my eyes, feeling my body shake as Hayden's lips pressed fervently along my neck.

I backed up and fell, naked, onto the bed. Still standing, Hayden watched me as he ripped open a condom. I recognized the hunger in his eyes, a reflection of my own that I'd felt so many times upon meeting that silver gaze. I remembered then the night we'd met, how I had later made myself come over and over again imagining that very look in his eyes and how much I wanted him to run it over my naked body.

The recollection took my breath away anew. Impulsively, I turned over as Hayden made a move toward the bed. I heard the duplicate intakes of breath as the inner exhibitionist in me seemed to break free, making me rise to my knees and drop my cheek against the mattress. I arched my back, wanting not only for them to get an unobstructed view of my naked pussy but also for Hayden to enter me that way, the way I'd imagined him doing so many times.

I felt him on the bed behind me. With a primal grunt, Hayden grabbed my hips and pushed into me as I gasped, spreading my knees wider as I felt my own wetness drip down my thighs.

I turned my face to Chris. His straining erection poked out of his open jeans, his eyes fastened to where Hayden's and my bodies connected. The hand resting on his cock held the slightest tension only I would recognize. He was holding back.

His gaze slid to mine, and my pussy jumped at the carnal desire I saw there. "Spank her," he said suddenly, his voice hoarse. "She loves that."

And that's when I heard it. I knew that pitch, that particular way Chris sounded when he was so turned on that he was having trouble keeping his composure. I'd heard it many times, in public, in private, at expected times and unexpected times. But I always knew what it meant.

Any trace of a question I had felt about Chris's comfort or security or desire dissolved when I heard that tone. I let out a shriek as Hayden complied, his hand connecting with my ass as I buried my face in the pillow in front of me, nearly dizzy with lust and desire and ecstasy. Hayden spanked me again, and again, and again, until I was so frenzied I hardly knew what was going on. Then he reached beneath me and brushed my clit, and I gyrated against his fingers frantically as I came, gripping the pillow that muffled my scream.

My body went limp as I finished. Hayden turned me over and knelt between my legs, and I looked up at him, breathing heavily. His gray eyes looked into mine, the heated yearning I had seen in them so many times merging with a carnal satisfaction as he slipped back inside me. I sighed and closed my eyes.

Hayden fucked me slowly as I ran my hands over my breasts. I moved them languidly, feeling my skin in a more intimate way than I ever remembered doing, connecting with my own body as much as with the other two in the room with me. Suddenly I felt in a state of utter vulnerability. I felt fragile, but not in a physical sense. Lying there naked with Hayden above me, Chris to my left, the caring and respect and openness I knew was in the room, my breath stopped in my throat. I felt tears come forth and didn't know how to hide them.

I turned my head away, unsure if either of them was looking at me. I didn't want them to think I was upset or that something was wrong, and I felt a vague, inexplicable embarrassment at feeling so strongly something I didn't even know how to describe.

The tears evaporated, and I looked back at Chris. He smiled at me this time, arousal combined with the tenderness and affection of the whole of the three and a half years we had shared together, telling me how much he loved this and how much he loved me all at once. The embarrassment vanished. I realized part of what I was feeling was gratitude and a monumental relief that Chris understood this, that he didn't feel intimidated, that he realized that what was happening was no threat to how I felt about him or my commitment to him or our relationship. That it was enhancing rather than diminishing anything.

I closed my eyes, the warmth rushing through my body making me reach out. Hayden interlaced his fingers with mine, and I opened my eyes. He smiled at me, too, the understanding in his gray eyes reflecting some of the same gratitude I experienced. I arched my back, meeting his slow thrusts, and his breath sharpened. I felt myself close to coming again as he lowered his body onto mine, his lips working their way up my neck to my ear.

Goose bumps sprayed over my body as he whispered into it. "Do you know how long I've fucking wanted this, wanted *you?*" The words seemed to shoot physically through me, my body responding involuntarily as I pushed against him, taking his thrusts deeper as I remembered all the times I had wanted Hayden inside me exactly as he was now, to be spread open below him, inviting him to take me however he wanted to. He kept whispering as I came again, the sound that ripped through my voice coming from my very center as he pressed my hands against the mattress, his fingers squeezing mine until I stilled.

My breath shuddered as the climax subsided. Hayden fucked me harder then, rising back up on his knees and grasping my thighs for traction. Out of the corner of my eye, I saw Chris stand and approach me in one fluid motion. I turned my head as he reached me, and his cock and my lips met as in a kiss, his flesh sliding seamlessly into the warm, wet haven of my mouth. I looked up at him with love, swirling my tongue around his length as he ran a hand through my hair.

Hayden's breath quickened, and his hands clutched me harder. I spread my legs farther for him, moaning against Chris as Hayden pounded into me. Chris started to push his cock in and out of my mouth, kneading one of my breasts as his other hand tightened on my hair. Hayden reached up to grip my waist and gasped as he came, thrusting hard and deep as his fingers dug into my flesh.

I closed my eyes as I felt overcome, centering for a moment to take in everything I was receiving. Hayden exhaled deeply as his body jerked, and I opened my eyes, pulling away from Chris for a moment to meet Hayden's silver gaze as I clenched my pussy around him.

I turned and took Chris's cock back in my mouth, knowing both of them were watching me as I sucked it hungrily. He thrust a little harder as his breath quickened, and I felt the first spurt of come on my tongue just as Hayden pulled out of me. Chris groaned as he shot his load into my mouth, and I rested a hand on his thigh, swallowing everything he gave me.

Finally he finished. I let his cock fall from my mouth and gave him the same smile he'd given me moments before from across the room.

Hayden, now dressed, sat on the bed as Chris zipped up his jeans. Only I was still naked, lying still under the gazes of both men as the air in the room calmed down once again. Myriad feelings, both expected and unexpected, moved inside me like a kaleidoscope. I hadn't anticipated feeling as close to Chris as I ever had, experiencing a level of trust that was unique, that had never been there before. And I felt an expansion, a freedom evoked not just by sexual satiation but by surrender, the surrender by all three of us to something unknown, something that could seem threatening but held the potential for something more, something unseen, something I had just experienced and didn't yet know how to describe.

Perhaps most of all, I felt astonished by the groundedness, openness and self-possession the willingness to even consider what had just taken place had required from both Hayden and Chris. The poignancy I'd experienced seeing them talking at Sarah's party magnified exponentially, and a lump formed in my throat as I marveled at the extraordinariness they had displayed.

Then I remembered what I knew about each man—in one case quite a bit and in the other a strong impression—and it didn't seem so surprising anymore.

IT'S GOTTA BE FATE

Jennifer Peters

The ad I posted online looking for a friend with benefits was very straightforward: *Submissive female looking to break her unlucky streak by dominating a new partner. No strings attached.* After breaking up with Kevin two years earlier, I'd fallen into a habit of only bedding other guys like him, guys who were dominant in the bedroom but couldn't commit, emotionally, to more than the occasional fling. I figured the only way to find someone who fit my needs was to change my tactics. I was never going to get over Kevin—who I had long ago decided needed to be gotten over, even if he was the love of my life—if I kept looking for guys who were exactly like him.

I used a new email address to post the ad online, and I listed my name as Anne to keep anyone from figuring out who I was. Just in case. And then the replies started pouring in. Some of them were a little creepy, some too romantic, but one in particular caught my attention. A guy who shared a first name with my ex replied that he was looking for a dominant woman to break his attraction to submissive females, and he thought we could easily help each other out of our unlucky romantic cycles. We exchanged a few emails discussing our kinky proclivities, and after we'd determined that we had similar sexual preferences, we set up a date to meet. Coffee would come first, and if we hit it off, we'd proceed to a room I'd already rented at a nearby hotel. I figured even if we didn't seem compatible in person, at least I'd get a night away from home in a posh hotel room. It seemed like a perfect plan to me.

The coffee shop was empty when I arrived on Saturday evening, and I ordered a latte and claimed a table. I was twenty minutes early, with plenty of time to enjoy some soothing chai and do some people watching. As the time for my meeting with the new Kevin approached, I turned my attention to the door, noting every person who came in and wondering if any of them were him. We'd agreed to use our travel mugs as identifiers and had exchanged photos of the cups in advance of our meeting. Mine was hot pink with a picture of a bulldog in a polka-dot dress on the front. His was orange camouflage. But no one was entering with his signature mug. I hoped he was just late and not standing me up, but I had no way of knowing. We hadn't exchanged phone numbers, wanting to protect our identities for as long as possible.

When I looked at the clock and saw that he was already ten minutes late, I started to think I'd been ditched. I was about to get up and leave when the café's door opened and in walked my ex. *Great*, I thought. *On top of the humiliation of being stood up, I now have to face my ex. This day couldn't get any worse.* Except, of course, it could. He spotted me and, like a deer in headlights, froze where he was and gaped at me for far longer than was polite. And that's when I saw it. In his right hand was an orange camouflage coffee cup.

Fuck my life! I screamed in my head. Of course the person I wanted to get over would be the one to answer my ad and say exactly what I wanted to hear. Of course that would happen. Because that was just the way my life worked. Two steps forward, three steps back. That dance had defined my relationship with Kevin for five years. Why shouldn't it apply now that I was no longer involved with him?

With a deep sigh I held up my pink mug and crooked my mouth into as much of a smile as I could stand to offer. I couldn't even begin to imagine how this was going to play out, but a part of me was extremely curious. After all, it wasn't our sexual chemistry that had led to our split.

Kevin approached slowly, almost nervously, shaking his head the whole time, clearly in as much shock as I was. "So, I guess we should've exchanged photos first," he said, and I laughed.

"Like that would've done us any good?" I asked. He looked at me curiously. "Please, we both would've shown up anyway. At least out of curiosity. And I'm willing to bet you're horny. You're *always* horny."

That made him crack a smile. "Well, you've got me there," he said. "I am always horny. Especially when I get around you."

I still couldn't believe it was Kevin sitting in front of me; that he was the mystery orange coffee mug. I ignored his attempt at flattery and looked him square in the eye as I said, "So, since we both showed up, what do we do now? Because I was serious in that ad. I want to dominate someone. And you did say in your email that you were looking to submit to the right girl."

A small part of me expected him to throw in my face the way I'd told him after our breakup that we'd never fuck again. He had always liked to watch me eat my words, so why wouldn't he get some joy out of it now that he had a chance? Another part of me, however, knew he wasn't kidding when he said he was always horny. I couldn't remember a date when we didn't end up tangled in the sheets.

"You said you wanted to break your bad luck with dominant men by taking charge, and I want to break my own streak of only going for girls who will submit to me," he said. "We might as well just do it. At least this way we know the sex will be good."

He had a point.

"Fine. Forget the coffee, then. Let's get to the hotel and get this over with," I demanded.

"That's my girl," he laughed, and I couldn't help smirking at the irony. In all our years together, he'd always been the one making the demands, and I'd always been the one tagging along after him. Funny how things were coming full circle.

The minute we walked into the hotel room, I did my best to forget who it was I'd be dominating and get right into my role. It was a lot easier than I'd expected it to be. I'd left a few essentials in the room when I'd checked in before going to the café, and after shedding my coat, I picked up the riding crop I'd bought for the occasion. I didn't think I'd use it much, but it helped me look the part, and that's what I cared most about—feeling like a domme, even if I didn't behave exactly like one.

After demanding that Kevin strip for me—which, I'll admit, I enjoyed for all sorts of reasons, the first and foremost being that I'd always loved looking at his body—I demanded that he then remove my clothes as well. "Slowly," I ordered. "I want sensual, not clumsy!" He'd always been a fan of going fast, so I thought this would be a nice change. And dear god, it was! With gentle hands he unbuttoned my blouse, one button at a time, and then peeled it open, exposing my bra. He slid the shirt carefully down my arms, his fingertips trailing over my skin as more of my body was exposed, and I got goose bumps. When he moved to take off my skirt next, I stopped him. "No, I don't think so," I said. "I've changed my mind. I want you to take off my panties next."

He obediently got on his knees and worked his hands up under my skirt until he reached the lacey edges of my panties. He inched his fingers under the leg bands and pulled the skin-tight material away from my body before starting to slide my panties down my legs. His touch was light, and he kept looking up at me to make sure he was doing exactly what I wanted. I was impressed that Kevin had it in him to be so accommodating, and even though he was doing an exceptional job, I really wanted to punish him. After he ate my pussy. I wasn't going to change my mind about that. If there was one thing he'd always done right, it was eating my cunt. So that's what I ordered him to do next.

Without hesitating, he said a brief, "Yes, Ma'am," and then ducked beneath my skirt and got right to work. I felt his breath on my cunt first, and I shivered in anticipation. When Kevin's tongue made contact, it took no more than a single lick to have me quivering in delight. His tongue worked its way between my slick folds and parted them farther. It felt like my lips were stage curtains, and a nervous actor was running his hand along the material as he walked across the stage. As his tongue slipped up and down my slit, my lips parted and came together in a slow, erotic way, and while a part of me craved a harsh tongue-fuck, I was enjoying this method of pussy-eating much more. My grip tightened on the handle of my crop as I moaned with pleasure. I was receiving the most intense, most enjoyable pussy-licking of my life, and I could hardly contain my desire to fuck. But a good domme doesn't fuck right away, I reminded myself, and I continued to savor the tongue-bath I was being treated to.

When I could no longer take the slow and sensual licking, I

pulled myself together enough to start beating the crop's leather tongue against Kevin's bare ass. "Fuck my pussy!" I cried. He started to move out from under my skirt, but I hiked the material up around my waist and shouted at him. "No, you fool!" I said. "Use your tongue. Fuck me with your mouth!" I continued hitting his ass with the crop, occasionally missing my aim and hitting him with the shaft instead of the tongue. It seemed to get my point across much quicker, actually, so it wasn't really an issue.

Kevin's tongue went from soft to hard, and he began jabbing my pussy with it, sometimes fucking me, and other times poking at my sensitive clit. I couldn't decide which was the more orgasm-inducing move, him thrusting his tongue between my lips or punishing my little clit. The combination of the two, I knew, spelled certain climax. And when I came a minute later, flooding his mouth with my copious juices, it didn't seem to matter whether his tongue had been between my folds or pressed against my clit, because either way, I was experiencing one incredibly intense orgasm!

As Kevin tried to draw out my orgasm with more tongue-fucking, I continued to slap his ass with my crop, not even trying to aim. It wasn't possible to focus on anything except taking pleasure from Kevin's deliciously talented mouth.

The crop slipped from my fingers as I relaxed after my climax, and I had to dig my fingers into Kevin's hair to keep my balance. I took several deep breaths, trying to regain focus, and when I could see straight once more, I lifted a high heel–clad foot and pushed the sole against his shoulder, moving him away from me. With Kevin out from between my thighs, my skirt fell back into place, and I demanded that he now remove it. He worked fast, his deft fingers quickly undoing the small hook closure and pulling down the zipper. I shimmied a bit as he wiggled the tight skirt down my hips, and then stepped gingerly out of the circle of cloth when it hit the floor.

By now I really wanted to fuck Kevin, our role-play having made me as horny as ever, but I wasn't ready to give up the sense of power I felt as I topped him. I wrapped a hand in his thick hair and turned sharply in my heels, marching to the bed a few feet away. I'd always loved when he pulled my hair, and he'd spent more than a few nights dragging me around our apartment by my mane. It never failed to get my juices flowing, and I'd always wondered if it would have the same effect on him. From the way he moaned when I pulled, I sensed that it did. Next, I ordered him onto the bed. Once he was spread-eagle, I reached under the pillow nearest me and pulled out a handful of silk ties. Fittingly, Kevin himself had left them at my place when we'd been dating, and now I was going to tie him up with them. Our little role-play game was getting more interesting by the minute.

I tied his hands together at the wrists before tying them to the headboard, and then I bound his ankles. He wouldn't be able to do anything that I didn't allow, not even if he tried. Touching me would be impossible, too, and I knew that would drive him absolutely crazy. It was the perfect torture!

Climbing onto the bed, heels still on, I straddled Kevin's hips while facing away from him. He loved my ass, but he loved my tits more and could never refrain from fondling and sucking them when we played. Now he wouldn't even be able to watch them as I fucked myself on his hard prick. Just thinking about how much he was going to hate that brought an evil gleam to my eye, I was sure, and I couldn't help but let out one quiet, wicked giggle.

I sank onto his cock and groaned as his length filled me. He'd always been the perfect size to accommodate me, and I had really missed riding him the past couple of years. Without another thought about what he might be thinking or feeling, I began to fuck him. I slid up and down his hard shaft, for once not caring if he was sharing in my pleasure. I did only what felt good for me, my hips moving in figure eights only when I needed the G-spot sensations, and my pelvis grinding against his only when my clit needed attention. I allowed myself to get lost in the sensations, and when I thought it would help to use some fingers to frig my clit and bring myself off faster, I did it without worrying what sort of message that might send my lover. Because for now, at least, he wasn't my lover—he was my slave.

Kevin had never failed to make me come when we were together, but I found that the climax I had while topping him was extremely different from the ones he'd given me while he was leading the show. My pussy throbbed in a whole new way, and I couldn't remember ever feeling so impassioned from riding him. My climaxes had always been better with Kevin on top, but now, letting myself go and just taking my pleasure from him without asking, I could finally understand the appeal of being on top and just riding. It was incredible!

My cunt spasmed around his cock a dozen times as I came, but he didn't even ask if he could have his release. He'd caught on quickly, and he knew he wouldn't be allowed to come until I told him he could.

When my second climax died down, I spun around on top of him, never removing myself from his cock, and began to ride him all over again, this time offering him a full-frontal view of my tits. It drove him crazy to see my nipples swaying in front of his face and not be able to suck them, and I knew it. He began moaning and whimpering, begging me to untie him so he could attack my breasts the way he liked. "Please," he pleaded.

"I just...I need...I have to have your tits!" He wouldn't stop begging, and the more he wanted them, the more I teased him. I grabbed my breasts in my hands and jiggled them, then shook them right in front of his face. "Just let me lick one!" he cried. "You have to give me one lick. Just a taste!" He tried sticking his tongue out to reach a nipple and even pulled his hands against the ties to try to grab a tit, but to no avail. He would just have to watch and wait his turn—if I even gave him a turn.

The more I teased Kevin, the more aroused I became, and soon I felt my third orgasm bubbling inside me. The sensations were overwhelming me, and I wasn't sure I'd have the energy for another round, so I told him to come with me. "Come now or not at all!" I shouted. His willpower gave out then, and he came, filling my cunt. I felt his dick throbbing as he pumped into me, and then my pussy spasmed and I came with him. The release I felt as I came this time was indescribable, and I threw my head back and screamed with delight.

As I slumped down against him, I reached up to untie his hands. After catching my breath, I unbound his ankles, too. Then we just lay there for a few minutes in utter silence. In the years we'd spent together, I'd never felt as close to him as I did in that moment. There had always been a barrier between us, and I was starting to think it was all because of our inability to switch roles in the bedroom—and in the rest of our relationship. Without thinking, I turned to him, grabbed a lock of hair in my fist, pulled him to me and kissed him. Our first kiss in two years, it was fiery and full of passion. And it was full of something else, too: promise.

"You know," he said, when I let him go and pushed him onto his back, "maybe we should give it another try." I looked at him, wondering if he meant the sex or... "Our relationship," he clarified quickly. "We ended up here, together. Maybe it was for a reason."

I thought about it for a few seconds, wondering what the right decision was. *Hell, it can't end any worse than last time*, I thought. I knew I still loved him, and that he'd never stopped loving me, either. And something about the way we'd ended up together because of that crazy ad I'd placed... Well, I wasn't one to believe in destiny, but who really knows? *Here goes nothing*, I told myself.

"Us, in bed together after all this time?" I said, gesturing at our bodies now angled toward each other under the sheets. "It's gotta be fate."

HOOKED

Ariel Graham

For three days, Ricki had stared at the hook. It was a simple enough thing, so basic neither she nor Jody noticed it during the endless job of moving into the new house.

"Short moves are worse," said her sister Thea, safely ensconced in Southern California and well away from the disaster occurring in Northern Nevada. "You think you can do it easily. You don't stock up on boxes. You try to set things up as you go. You deny the fact that you're going to be eating microwaved Ramen for months because you can't find the saucepans that have been packed in a box marked 'drindle.'"

"What's drindle?" Ricki asked, dangling packing peanuts on a strip of packing tape to entertain the cats.

"Exactly," Thea said.

The move went in fits and starts. Moving from a desert cow-town-turned-suburb back into Reno meant a forty-mile drive one way. With Jody working in Reno and Ricki working from home, it meant they both dropped off a load of boxes once a day and nothing much else got done. They weren't in their twenties anymore and while they might have some time before forty hit, they got tired faster and summer in the desert was hot.

And Thea was right. It was harder to move a short distance. They didn't want to keep renting U-Hauls and with the one house a rental from friends and the other they were leaving already sold to people who wouldn't move in for another month, they had time.

Having time stretched out the agony.

Which meant they'd been tired for months. Ricki would lie in bed in the morning until the very last minute, watching through the arch into the master bath while Jody showered and shaved and came back to bed, naked, dark, gorgeous. Droplets of water shone in the dark hair on his chest and between his legs. He'd come back to kiss her before he got dressed but the kiss didn't usually lead to anything.

When they finally got moved, over the aptly-named Labor Day weekend, they planned to initiate each room of the house.

Later.

And later led to housewarming and graphic arts deadlines for Ricki and long hours on the construction site for Jody.

She finally noticed the hook in the corner of the new bedroom while Jody was taking a shower one morning in the connected-but-separate master bath. As steam billowed into the bedroom and birds practiced octaves in the apple tree out back, Ricki stretched, her hands roaming without intent over her own mostly flat belly, down lower to cover her mons, lightly teasing the edges of her own clit, but she stopped before actually separating her lips. If they had energy. Maybe over the weekend. But not alone. It always seemed like a waste. She opened her eyes and glanced around the ceiling of her new bedroom. In the empty corner of the big new bedroom where no furniture had been set up yet, she saw a shadow on the ceiling.

Her first instinct was to jolt upright. Her idle moments of cuddling with her head on Jody's shoulder and her eyes half open and gazing around had found them far too many spiders over the years and far too many nights of Ricki saying, "No, I can't just turn the light out and forget it, there's a spider on the ceiling, here's a tissue, just kill it."

And this thing she saw now was *big*.

And not moving.

She pushed the sheet back and padded naked across the carpet to the corner, raised up on tiptoes and squinted.

Not alive. Not anything that ever had been.

"What are you *doing*?" Jody asked and she jolted hard enough to snap her teeth together. She hadn't heard him come up behind her at all, stepping from the bathroom linoleum onto the carpet. The tile and hardwood of the last house had given her warning.

"Sorry," Jody said. His hands on her shoulders were shower warm and a little damp. "I thought you heard me."

"It's a hook," Ricki said, as it suddenly came into focus the way hidden image pictures did.

"Yessss," Jody said in his "Thank you for stating the obvious; are you sure you're quite sane?" voice.

"Why would anyone—oh, for plants?" She turned her head to look at him and he had to look up to meet her eyes. Ricki started to drop down to flat feet and Jody caught her elbow and gently pushed her back up. She teetered, caught the wall with one hand and blinked at him.

"I like the line of your body," he said, and stepped completely behind her. "The *V* down to the waist, this beautiful ass—" He cupped it and squeezed, and Ricki, who had drawn in breath to point out she knew whose ass he meant, bit her lip instead. "Nice long legs. Why don't you just look back up at that hook? Like you want to reach it?"

And then, slightly smiling, bemused and a little embarrassed, she did. He ran his hands down her shoulders, along her back; ran his thumbs down the soft knobs of her spine; let his hands go warm and flat along her lower back, just along her hips, and spread his hands over her hips, pulled her to him; used his thumbs to separate her asscheeks. She felt him bend his legs so he fit tight against her, his cock pressed hard between her cheeks and against his belly. His hands came around and cupped her breasts, thumbs flicking, then pinching and pulling her nipples. She groaned, started to look away from the hook, felt their positions shift and looked back up at it.

"Good girl," he whispered, and she bristled for a minute, feeling whatever he'd meant it was somehow out of place. Degrading. Only—not quite. More—humiliating. As if he'd told her what to do and she'd done it and been awarded a treat, like a trained animal.

She liked it. She liked the thrill that ran through her, the flush of embarrassment. Jody bit her neck and, forgetting the hook, she turned in his arms. He pulled one leg over his arm and slid inside her as if they'd choreographed the movement. She grabbed hold of him, nails digging a little into his back as she struggled for balance.

"Carefully," he said. "Don't scratch me. You don't want a spanking, do you?"

Startled, she tried to answer, tried to move so she could see his face. In the next instant, their bodies pressed together so their weight caught her clit. Jody came seconds after she did and they clung together, Ricki's back against the wall, her hands still locked around his neck; Jody's hands on either side of her, supporting himself against the bedroom wall, just under the hook in the ceiling.

* * *

Later that day she went back into the bedroom, searching for the boxes, which had managed to get and remain packed despite the short easy move, for some of the things she'd packed absolutely last because she needed them most and most often—her running shoes. The teakettle. His keys.

The cats stared out from under the bed at her, identical striped gray creatures with gold eyes that harbored deep suspicion. She'd already moved them to a new house in a new city. Who knew what else she was capable of?

"Boys," she said, and tripped over a pair of jeans left unceremoniously on the floor. They were still moving, still settling in. She stopped, gathered them, stood and arched her back—and found herself staring at the hook again.

It had definitely led to a good time in the morning. Now she looked at it again, wondering. The corner would get some light, but she couldn't imagine it got enough light to make a plant happy. And it was a big hook. Thick, anyway, the metal as wide as the tongue that slid into the two parts of a gate latch to catch and close it. What kind of hanging plant got that heavy? When she looked closer, she saw the hook had been screwed in through an anchor, one of those things that went into the ceiling and fanned out, creating more—what? Tension? Tensile strength? "Holding capacity," Ricki said aloud, and stood on tiptoe to look closer, the way she had in the morning when Jody had come up behind her.

"Why don't you just look back up at that hook?" he'd asked. "Like you want to reach for it?"

She reached for it. On tiptoe, as if she could touch the ten-foot ceiling, she reached, with both hands. An image came to mind: her hands bound at the wrist, with some kind of silken cord, maybe like a curtain tie; something soft but strong enough to keep her bound, even if she struggled.

Would she struggle?

Ricki held her hands out toward the hook and imagined Jody standing behind her. "That's a good girl," he said. Such a condescending line, really. Like she was doing what she was told.

She'd have to do what she was told, wouldn't she? If he tied her up.

Somewhere down the hall in the den/her studio/the place where the box with all the cookbooks might be, her phone rang. Ricki's calves gave, dropped her back down to her heels. Alone, and fully dressed, she blushed, gave the hook a dark look and went fast up the hall to grab her phone.

At the end of the second day, she lay on her back with her hands laced behind her head, staring up at the ceiling. Jody lay beside her, up on one elbow, reading a thriller. The pages brushed her ribs every time he turned them but she felt too lazy to move. Her eyes went to the hook, her mind idle and uninterested in much of anything. One thought about the hook and then she switched to thoughts about what the next day would bring—Friday, lunch with a friend, meeting with a client, invoicing to do and some time to do her own painting—and the hook swam in and out of focus for her, now erotic, now a piece of hardware.

Ricki blinked and smiled at Jody, who gave her a slight smile as he turned another page, brushing her gently. Ricki closed her eyes. For a few moments, she thought of nothing, just on the verge of sleep. And then the hook was in her mind again and the way she'd thought it was a spider, and she opened her eyes and looked at every square inch of ceiling that she could see. Nothing. Okay. No spiders. Her eyes drifted back to the hook. She licked her lips. What if he tied her with something long enough so she could be on her knees. A truly submissive position. Of course she could do the obvious, there, but—

"What are you staring at?" Jody asked, twisting around so he could lie down beside her and share her point of view. "That hook again? It's just a hook!"

Tell him, she thought wildly. It's Jody. *Even if he doesn't want—he won't—he wouldn't say anything—*

He'd said she might need a spanking.

He was just kidding.

"Just thinking about the other morning," she said lightly, and felt the opportunity slip away.

She thought she could almost hear him grin. "I have to leave early tomorrow, but if you're *quick—*"

He threw the sheet off his lower body, showing off a very nice erection, hard, thick, pointing right at the ceiling when he lay back and suggested she "have her way with him."

That's halfway to what I was thinking, she thought, and moved so she could straddle his face. Usually just going down on Jody made her hot. Tonight she was already there.

"Hello there," Jody said, and his tongue flicked up across her clit. His aim was always perfect. His hands went to her hips and he pulled her close, sucking and licking alternately, taking his tongue from her clit to cunt, teasing her lips aside, dipping inside. She held still for a minute, her forearms braced against his thighs, just feeling before she lowered her head, slid her very open mouth as far down his cock as she could, then latched on, sucking hard, pulling her head up to slide the tension all the way up his shaft, swirl her tongue hard around the head, and repeat until he'd left off teasing her, breathing through his mouth, sliding two fingers inside her cunt in place of his tongue. Ricki arched her back, pressed against his hand, and he added his thumb to her clit. She gasped, slid down his cock again, as if she meant to swallow it, and began fucking him with her mouth as hard and fast as she could.

He filled her mouth and his hand stilled at that instant, fingers pushed as hard and far into her as they'd go, thumb resting against her clit so all she had to do was shift against him and she came, too, waves lapping across her body, shudders making her shiver as she licked the last of his come off his now ultrasensitive cock. For a breath, they both held still, muscles tense, then they collapsed against each other, Ricki giggling softly, and Jody had to clear his throat twice before he could properly say, "Come here."

She nestled against him, head in the hollow of his shoulder, and they dozed, contented, and through half-open eyes, Ricki watched the hook.

On the third day, Friday, she tried to think of ways to tell him. Everything they could do together, they'd done, no holds barred, and he constantly complimented her on her lack of inhibitions—and still she couldn't tell him her fantasies. The few that had been worked out over their years together had been accidental. Sometimes Jody guessed. Sometimes he just observed something she'd reacted to and built on it. Sometimes he was even dead wrong, she thought, remembering a sticky debacle with ice cream and whipped cream and other foods she hadn't wanted to eat again for months (and neither had he; plus who knew how hard it was to wash ice cream off bedclothes?) She'd never been able to tell him, though.

Friday morning he left early, gave her a kiss and headed off to work before she even managed to get out of bed.

Halfway though the morning, Ricki left off with her current work project and went into the bedroom to shower and go meet her friend for lunch. Dropping her shorts and T-shirt on the bed, she turned toward the master bath and stopped, staring again at the hook. Her fantasies kept growing. She imagined kneeling, hands pulled up on the cord attached to the hook that now seemed to be some kind of pulley system because when Jody forced her to her feet, the cord stayed taut. She imagined him making good on his promise to spank her (an offhand comment, she reminded herself, not a promise, but her eyes fluttered half closed and she swayed where she stood). Jody's hands would sweep down over her naked body while she stood, drawn up on tiptoes by her bonds, and then he'd draw back one hand and slap her bottom, leaving a stark red handprint against her white flesh. They'd both go still for a moment, considering, and then he'd push her forward, bending her over so the skin grew tight over her ass and thighs, and he'd start spanking her, a little slowly at first, but as her butt reddened and her breath shortened to little gasps, she'd hear him taking off his clothes and realize all this time she'd been naked and powerless and he'd still been dressed and—

Her phone rang and Ricki jolted, coming down to earth. Her breath came short and her cheeks were flushed. She reached one hand back and ran it over her own asscheek, wondering.

Who the hell hangs plants in a bedroom corner? And how big was it anyway, to require such a large hook?

Just how hard would someone have to tug against a rope tied there before one's husband had to fix a nasty spot in the ceiling where the hook had pulled out? And really, how hard could that be?

And then she had to hurry—rushed shower, ponytail, very little makeup; very little time. She got to lunch seven minutes late and the only thing Emma said was, "You look *great*. Having a good day?"

"I hope so," Ricki said.

* * *

She chickened out before Jody ever got home. Chickened out, decided again. Made up her mind. Became determined. Rehearsed what she'd say. Decided to go to a craft store or fabric store and buy the cord.

But surely twine would work as well until they could buy cord together? And what if she hated it? Artists and carpenters weren't made of money. Might as well try it first with something cheaper. She could always tell him later.

If she could ever tell him.

She wasn't going to think about it anymore.

She'd take the hook down over the weekend. Who the hell hangs plants in the corner of the bedroom where they don't get any light?

Then why was she in here again?

"You working?" Jody called through the house.

Ricki jumped. She hadn't heard his truck, or heard him come in, and had no idea it was after five.

"I am so hungry," she said, and went out of her studio to wrap her arms around him.

"Hello to you, too," he grinned before he kissed her.

"Did you bring food?" She'd had a salad for lunch because Emma was so damn thin it made her self-conscious to eat in front of her. Surely it was rude to eat in front of wraiths who could only choke down a few bites of celery? In her nonsexual fantasies, she sometimes dreamed of watching Emma eat an entire cheesecake.

"Was I supposed to bring food?" Jody asked.

"No, I'm just hopeful." She leaned back in his arms and grinned up at his dark brown eyes and tan face. He cocked his head at her and sawdust drifted down out of his hair. "If I take a shower, you could eat *me*."

"I might bite."

"Not that kind of eating."

"I might faint."

He rolled his eyes. "Have a nice sandwich while I take a shower and then if you cooperate"—he kissed her neck on each syllable of *cooperate*—"I'll take you out to dinner. Where do you want to go?"

"Somewhere with cheesecake," she said, and went to make a sandwich.

She did go down on him, sucking and nibbling up and down the sensitive edges of his cock, holding his balls loosely, until finally he growled and grabbed her and flipped her onto her back, joined her arms over her head against the mattress with one hand and used the other to guide himself into her. He fucked her roughly and she curled her legs up around his waist, drawing him deeper. When he moved she could see the hook in the corner.

He brought her to the edge of orgasm and went still. His weight still on her arms, he arched his back and pulled out of her until just the tip of his cock stayed inside her. Incensed, Ricki lunged at him with her hips. He slid back easily. She met his eyes, half amused, panting.

"What are you doing?"

He grinned and gestured behind him with a flip of his chin toward the far corner. "You have been staring at that thing for three days."

She shook her head and tried to interrupt.

"And we've had some *very* good sex in those last three days."

She closed her eyes and whimpered slightly, pushing her hips up at him again. He just didn't bother to move.

She subsided.

"I want to know what you're thinking."

"I can't," she said, and in that moment, meant it.

Jody slid all the way out of her and pressed himself against her side. One hand kept both of hers trapped. The other reached down and started tracing circles around her clit, faster and harder until she shuddered toward release. And then he stopped. And did it again. And kissed her neck and buried his face in her hair and whispered, "Tell me."

Saturday morning, they drove together to the craft store.

AFTERSHOCKS

Bella Andre

Celeste Maclean stood in the middle of the empty ten-by-fifteen storage unit, looked at all the crap she and her husband had accumulated during their marriage and wondered aloud, "Why the hell did we ever buy this stuff?"

All alone in the room, she wasn't expecting the answer, "We were hoping it could save us."

She barely stopped herself from whirling around in surprise. That raw, gravelly voice from behind her had once had the power to make her instantly wet, whether they were in line for sandwiches at the deli or already under the covers, with his breath moving across her clit as he teased her with sweet words.

"Darren." She said her soon-to-be ex-husband's name without looking at him. "What are you doing here?"

"Same as you. Figured it was time to decide what to keep. And what to let go."

She could feel him coming closer, the heat of him invading the small space, making her painfully aware of the fact that there were no windows and only one exit through a long, badly lit hallway.

He'd always been better with words than she had—his writer trumped her management consultant any day—and she knew he wasn't just talking about the inanimate objects.

Her heart squeezed—they'd been such good friends once, but being friends wasn't good enough, damn it!—and she forced herself to lock her wall of armor back into place.

"I don't want anything in here," she made herself say, her words dropping like metal bullets on the cement floor between them.

Jesus, even for me that was mean, she thought with the regret she couldn't contain, no matter how hard she tried. Who would have thought this was how love was going to end up... with bitter, final good-byes being hurled at each other in the middle of a cold storage unit.

Leave. She needed to leave.

Turning blindly away from him, she was halfway across the unit when the floor slipped out from beneath her. Darren was there to catch her before she could fall, his large hands circling her waist, his chest hard against her back.

Hating the nerves that had her slipping in her heels in front of the man she was leaving, she said, "I'm okay now. Thanks." But before she could pull away, all around them boxes started falling, lamps and pictures coming crashing down.

Darren pulled her down beneath the upright piano, covering her body with his as a huge earthquake shook the building. The tremors came so hard, and so close together, that although she could feel the hits that he was sustaining ricochet through his body even as he protected her, she couldn't do anything more than pull him closer. And then, a crash came that was so loud, so hard, she actually gasped in his arms as he murmured nonsense words to calm her, just like he always used to when she was crying over something.

Finally, there was silence, broken only by the sounds of their breathing and the beat of his heart drumming against her ear.

"Are you okay, Darren?"

He shifted slightly away from her and she instinctively pulled him tighter to her.

"Better now." His response rumbled from his chest to hers. "So much better now."

Oh, god. They'd just survived one hell of an earthquake in a room full of dangers and instead of crying, instead of freaking out, she was wet. Soaking through her panties from nothing but his arms, tight around her, his breath whispering over her ear.

She'd been looking for adventure, had been wanting to live on the edge for so long, that instead of frightening her, the earthquake had been foreplay.

That was why she knew that the biggest danger wasn't going to be from aftershocks and falling boxes. It was staying here, with Darren.

Because if she wasn't careful, she'd give in, and they'd be right back where they always had been. Back to good. But good wasn't good enough—not when she wanted fireworks and breathless need and desire so strong that pleasure was almost pain.

"Thank you for protecting me," she said, her voice, her movements, robotic as she made herself push away from the heat, the comfort, of Darren's arms. "I'm going to be late for an appointment," she lied. "I need to go."

He let her go, but she could feel the anger riding him, vibrating through his hand to hers as he helped her stand, as she got ready to bolt.

But when she looked over at the door, it was closed. "Did you shut the door?"

"No. The earthquake must have done it."

She rushed over to it, yanked on the handle with all her might. "We're locked in."

"Good."

His eyes blazed with a fire she'd only seen a couple of times during their five-year marriage and her heart responded by jumping behind her breastbone.

"It's not good," she protested, but her voice was breathier than it should have been. "We need to get out of here. You need to help me try to get this open."

But he didn't move toward her, just stood there in the middle of the room. "Not until you tell me why."

Her hands stilled on the door's metal handle. She knew what he was asking. But she'd already answered him a hundred times; first in person and then through lawyers.

"You know why." She was so frustrated by all of this that each of her words were clipped. "We're not compatible. We want different things."

He'd always dreamed of moving out to a ranch in the west. She thrived in the city. He was a dreamer, a writer who could spend hours on the fantasy worlds he built in his head. She was practical, a businesswoman to the core. Stupid her for ignoring the warning signs in those early years. Stupid her for thinking that initial spark was enough to last a lifetime.

"Stop lying to me, Celeste."

One second he was standing across the room, the next he was in front of her, his hands hard on her shoulders, his face ravaged by pain.

"At least have the courage to tell me the goddamned truth before you leave me forever."

"You're too gentle!" She was yelling back at him now, the words coming without any help from her brain. "I thought I was marrying a man. I thought I was marrying someone who would give me what I needed." She sneered. "I hate myself for being wrong. And I hate you for leaving me like this, so damn needy, feeling like I was sick and twisted for wanting things you would never dream of giving me."

His nostrils flared. "Are you telling me that you don't like gentle, Celeste? Are you telling me that you'd rather be with a man who hurts you?"

"No, damn it, that's not what I'm saying. Sometimes I like gentle. Of course I do. But sometimes," she tried to find the right words, "sometimes I wanted you to claim me. To make me yours. To completely lose control and stop making love to me and just fuck me instead."

His hands were a rough caress over her arms, down to her wrists, where he forced them behind her back and gripped them tightly in one hand. "You want a man who knows how to be aggressive? You want a man who makes you submit to him?"

"No. Not just anyone." The admission spilled from her mouth, just as her arousal was spilling between her thighs at his rough, possessive touch. "I wanted to submit to you."

"And I wanted to dominate you." His voice dropped to a dangerously low pitch. "Don't speak again unless I give you permission."

Her breath caught in her throat as she watched her husband transform before her very eyes into the man she'd dreamed of for so long. Using the leverage of her hands behind her back, he pulled her harder against him, her nipples pebbling against his chest.

"All these years, I held back for you."

She shivered as he leaned down and took one of her earlobes between his teeth. She gasped with surprise—and with more pleasure than she'd ever felt before—at the sensation of being captive to him as he bit down on her tender flesh.

"All these years, I thought loving you meant walking away from the darkness."

His lips, his tongue, his teeth found her neck, scraping the skin, making her legs tremble hard enough that his hands on her wrists were the reason she was still standing.

"So many nights I watched you sleep and thought you'd hate me if you knew who I really was. If you knew what I really wanted from you. If I ever slipped and tried to take what I needed from you."

She moaned out loud as his free hand came around a breast, his fingers finding her hard nipple beneath her bra and top, rolling, squeezing. He'd always been a tender lover, had always been focused on foreplay, had never ever touched her like this.

"Take it. Take me." The words rasped from her throat between the breaths she was only just managing to drag inside.

He spun her around so quickly she had no time to react, only to realize that he must have kicked out the piano bench and was sitting on it, with her sprawled facedown across his lap.

Her hands were still bound in his hand behind her back and it was pure instinct to struggle in his grip, even as warmth moved across her, into her, through every one of her cells.

I don't have to give him up.

The sweet thought came so fast she almost missed it, but then the crack of his palm across her ass had her losing the thread of any thoughts at all.

"Don't." He shoved up her skirt, took another shot at her ass with his palm coming hard onto her panties. "Speak." He ripped the lace from her skin. "Again." He shoved open her legs and slapped down on her exposed pussy. "Without." Two fingers thrust inside her, the rough glide softened by her slick arousal. "Permission."

She tried to swallow her whimper, her plea for more, but then his thumb came down over her clit and she was flying too high, too far, to have any self-control at all. She was only vaguely aware of him letting go of her wrists, of his hand moving between his thighs and her chest to her breasts. All she knew was that she was finally there, that her husband was finally taking her to the peak that had always been just out of reach.

"Don't you dare come yet."

His words pierced her orgasmic haze a split second before she disobeyed him.

"I can't help—"

His hand cracked down on her ass again, making her gulp down the rest of her sentence.

"You're going to have to help it."

She was almost able to control herself again, and then his hard words had her on the verge of falling over the edge. It didn't help that right then the ground shook again, the aftershock moving his fingers deeper into her, pressing against her G-spot so perfectly she knew she was a goner.

But then—she didn't know if she should thank god or be stupendously pissed off—he was moving her again, lifting her from his lap so that she was kneeling between his legs. Her clit throbbed, her breasts ached.

And she was happy.

So goddamned happy she couldn't believe it.

She was about to reach for his pants when she realized he hadn't given her permission to do so. Licking her lips uncertainly—and loving the uncertainty—she looked up into his dark, heated gaze.

"Good girl."

His praise warmed her, had her thrusting her breasts into his hands like a cherished pet. He rewarded her by rolling her nipples between his thumb and fingers.

"Now be a bad girl."

She didn't have to think about it, was instantly there with her mouth on the snap of his jeans, pulling it open with her teeth. Using her tongue, she grabbed hold of the zipper, the metal taste strange in her mouth as she pulled it down, a slow slide over the huge bulge of his cock. Her mouth watered with the urge to taste him, his clean male scent already driving her crazy. And it was tempting, so damn tempting, to take his cotton-covered shaft into her mouth. But she didn't want just part of him, didn't want anything separating them anymore.

Not a thin layer of cotton...and not all of the desires they'd hidden from each other for so long.

Her teeth made short work of his boxers and then his thick, hard cock was right where she wanted it. Right where she needed it. A breath away from her mouth, until she took that breath and inhaled him along with the oxygen.

"Jesus, baby." His groan of pleasure, his guttural words, had her heart swelling beneath her breastbone. "You've never taken me this far."

She'd always wanted to deep-throat him, but he'd said he hadn't wanted to hurt her, and together neither of them had gotten a damn thing they'd wanted. Well, she was taking it all from him now, her delight all the bigger for the knowledge that everything she was so selfishly taking would come back to him doubled for his pleasure.

He hadn't given her permission to cup his balls, to scratch her fingernails against the patch of skin behind them, but she was too busy enjoying herself to worry about a punishment that might be coming. The salty-sweet taste of him shot into the back of her throat. It wasn't a full-blown orgasm, but it was enough for her to know that she had him right where she wanted him.

Only, she hadn't counted on her husband, on this man she was only starting to know after being with him for half a decade, because instead of letting her suck on his dick until he exploded down her throat, his hands shifted from her breasts to her armpits and he lifted her up with such force, her feet actually came off the ground for a moment. And then he was turning her again, pushing her up against the piano so hard that it started playing, music clanging to life in the middle of four walls, in the middle of broken possessions nobody had ever cared about, in the middle of love coming back to life.

"Put your hands up on the wall."

She couldn't believe her hands were shaking as she pressed them flat against the wall.

"No matter what happens, no matter what I do, I don't want you to move a damn muscle."

She expected him to take her hard and fast, doing with his cock just what he'd done with his fingers a little while earlier. But when she felt his breath against the back of her knees, she realized she'd underestimated him.

Again.

"Remember," he said in a soft voice that was all the more potent for the lack of threat behind it, "don't come."

His tongue lashed against the seam behind her knee and she forced herself to press tighter against the piano instead of into her husband's tongue. Working his way slowly up first one leg and then the other, he licked her hamstring, stopping both times at her ass. Her rear still tingled from the spanking he'd given her earlier, and she had to bite her tongue between her teeth to keep herself from begging for him to touch her there.

And all the while, her juices pooled between her legs, to the point where she could actually feel them starting to trail down the insides of each thigh, a trail of desire, of pure lust for the man she'd pledged her love to on a sunny August day in the middle of a vineyard. Five years ago. She'd had so many hopes, so many dreams.

Hopes that she could finally hand over to the man who she now knew would take care of making her dreams all come true.

"So wet."

She felt him lick at her juices, getting close to her pussy, but never actually touching her labia, her astonishingly swollen clit.

"So pretty."

He licked at her other thigh.

"All for me."

The softness left his voice, replaced by the dark lash of desire. And possession.

"Only for me."

She should have been prepared for the sudden, flat stroke of his tongue across her labia, for the hard thrust of it into her pussy, but no one had ever fucked her like this. Especially not her husband.

Her weight all but fell onto the piano, causing the symphony to play again just as he shifted his mouth once more and sucked her clit in between his lips.

His earlier command, *Remember, don't come,* blinked like a neon sign in front of her eyes, but it was quickly being overshadowed by the fireworks he was lighting off one at a time between her legs, and she knew there was no way she could stop herself from coming. Not anymore. Not even to please her husband.

Her sinfully sweet, deceptively dangerous husband.

And then she felt, more than heard, his words, "Come for me," against her mound.

Pathetically grateful, loving him more than she ever had before, she ground herself against his lips, his tongue, his teeth, intent on nothing more than riding out this beautifully unexpected orgasm.

But, still, she hadn't reckoned on her husband. Because even as she was still held in the grip of her climax, he was pulling her down to the floor, over his throbbing cock, his mouth moving from her pussy to her mouth between breaths.

And before she even had time to come down from the first explosion, her sheer pleasure at the way his cock was stretching her—claiming her all over again—had her riding him, riding toward the next wave, until his hands clamped down hard on her hips, holding her still.

She blinked at him, seeing the same face, the same eyes and hair and cheekbones of the man she'd married. He was a beautiful man, had always been breathtaking, but as he held her so firmly in his hands, as he loved her the way she'd always wanted to be loved, she finally felt safe with him.

Like she was finally at home with the man she'd been living alone with for so many years.

"I love you, Darren."

Without letting her move a muscle, without thrusting any deeper into her, she felt him begin to come, a hot blast of semen deep in her womb setting off another round of fireworks in her belly.

"I love you, Celeste."

She never wanted to let go of him, would have happily stayed there on this lap, her legs wrapped around his waist, her arms around his neck, her cheek to his forever.

A chunk of plaster fell onto her shoulder, quickly followed by Darren's, "Oh, fuck. I think the ceiling is going to come down on us."

She knew she should be worried, but her limbs were all buttery and loose. "We can just hide under the piano again. We could do all of it over again."

She loved the rumble of his laughter, but then he was picking her up and standing in front of her just as another chunk—a bigger chunk—of the ceiling landed two inches away.

"Ready to go home?"

She knew what he was asking, but she had to ask a question of her own before she could give him her answer. "No more hiding? No more pretending?"

Finally, he kissed her, a kiss full of the kind of honest love she'd been waiting for her whole life.

"Never again. Only love, sweetheart." His wicked half smile had her catching her breath again. "And taking care of you the way I should have been all along."

She wanted him to take care of her again, right then and there, but when another aftershock rocked the room again, he took her hand in his and put them both over the door handle.

"One. Two." Her eyes locked with his and she knew he was loving their first adventure as a real married couple as much as she was. "Three."

Together they yanked open the metal door, then ran like hell out of a crumbling building that had brought their crumbling marriage back to new life.

SECRET PLACES

Adele Haze

When the boy comes, he screams like a creature pierced with a predator's claw; his face contorts into something beyond joy and pain. Marian's fingertips can't get a grip against his sweat-slick biceps, so she throws her arms around him and holds him in a full-body embrace as he rides out the storm. His calming breath sounds like sobs, and in his eyes she can read the heart-melting tenderness that keeps her hoping, keeps her hanging on.

He says: "Oh, hon." He gently lowers himself to rest against her, cheek to flushed cheek.

He doesn't say, "I love you." And neither does she, though surely he must know.

She thinks of Dan as "the boy" because that's how she first knew him: the boy busking in the long subway underneath King's Cross Station, his music a daily theme song to her evening commute. Because she can't play an instrument, she could never tell if he was any good. All she knew, even back then, was that his music made her soul unclench. His voice was chocolate and velvet, but not so special that he'd ever be a stage sensation. It worked on her, though. From time to time, she dropped coins in his guitar case, and fancied herself a patron of the arts. Most times, she was more broke than her City suit implied and took pleasure in his songs with no recompense.

In early January, when frozen rain hammered down for days on end, turning into black slush underfoot, she noticed, unsettled, that the boy wasn't there to serenade her out of London with Bob Dylan covers. She suspected he'd been missing for a few days before she noticed.

Was she worried? She doesn't know, but she fancies now that she did fret for a while. It must have been the unconscious worry, she thinks, that made her notice him in the Starbucks queue upstairs and made her bold enough to offer him a drink.

His spoken voice had safe, middle-class vowels, and instead of the hipster coffee she'd expected to pay for, he asked for a mug of tea.

They talked about London: a Victorian monster hiding still behind the city of air and glass. They talked about the bewilderment of growing up; she was his elder by two years, but he had walked out of the parental home when she still had a monthly allowance, and so her seniority didn't count for much. They probed the soft edges of getting-to-know-you topics, and continued to do this over extravagant burgers in the freezing St. Pancras terminal. Marian forgot to be embarrassed by her appetite. She took pleasure in watching the boy fold fat fries into his mouth. When finally she suggested that it was time she took herself home to bed, he said, "My bed is nearer."

Although his voice rose at the end, making it sound like a question, there was no question in her mind that his bed was where she wanted to be.

* * *

The boy's housemate is a wild-haired creature called Nathaniel. He wears grandfather braces and horn-rimmed specs, and studies physical chemistry—seemingly at all hours. He has a wealthy boyfriend who never stays over, preferring sex on clean hotel sheets. At first, Marian had been embarrassed to be the recipient of these details of Nathaniel's life, but promptly realized that in a house where each of the two rooms was the size of a Covent Garden Station elevator, oversharing was a good cure for awkwardness.

Nathaniel was quick to let Marian know how much he approved of her sudden presence. On the morning of her third or fourth visit, they drank coffee in the kitchen while Dan showered, and Nathaniel said, "You're really good for him. Particularly after Tanya."

Mouth bitter—because of the cheap coffee, she assured herself—Marian said, "We haven't got as far as Tanya."

"You will," said Nathaniel, unconcerned by his slipup. "As soon as he can talk about her without tearing out clumps of hair. It's only been, like, a month." He gave her a disconcerting wink.

He often winks at her. She doesn't like it.

Dan admits that his housemate is demonstrably incompatible with any of his other friends, and this isn't hard to believe.

One evening she stumbled into the kitchen; her neck was aching from trying to catch a glimpse of Dan as he pressed into her from behind. She found Nathaniel playing at a tea party with glove puppets. She forgot to be embarrassed about the sex noises she'd been failing to suppress: she felt he had a more weighty cause for embarrassment.

Later, Dan rested his head against her, and she played with his hair, nut-colored coils glued together with sweat.

"It's the trick for survival in cities, isn't it?" she said. "If you're going to live packed together with strangers, you find the few oddballs whose weirdness you don't mind, and who don't mind your weirdness in return."

"Mmm," he said. "Or you could try being rich."

"Or that." She gave his hair a little yank. He yipped in response, and turned around to lick her hand.

She stroked his face. "I like your weirdness," she said.

With her free arm wrapped around him, she felt the boy tense.

"Any weirdness…in particular?" he asked with palpable caution. She could tell she'd inadvertently poked his soft place, and although she was dying to find out what it was, she made an effort to stop herself from prying.

"All of them, actually, but come to think of it, your musical snoring is kind of endearing."

This was the right response, because Dan relaxed against her and soon turned around for some nuzzling and lazy, tired kisses.

She wondered about the secret place he was protecting from her. Maybe Tanya had found it first: a Bluebeard's room inside the boy's head. Marian tried to imagine a part of him she couldn't love, and failed. She discovered with surprise that she was thinking about love and knew it was right, but she kept it to herself: her own soft, protected place.

Their ritual goes like this. On her way back from work, Marian stops to hear the boy play. He always notices her right away, but always finishes the song. They kiss and hold each other, the rush-hour crowd pouring past them toward the stations outside. Some days he says, "See you tomorrow?" She says, "Of course." He plays a song she likes, T. Rex, or the Doors, or something by Nick Cave that's monumentally unsuitable to be a serenade. Then she allows the crowd to carry her away.

Some days he says, "Do you want to come back to mine?" She says, "Of course." She goes upstairs to wait for him in a coffee shop, stays there until all the songs are played and the people torrent has died down. They go back to his house, holding hands through four zones of the underground line. Sometimes they remember to get food. Sometimes they feast on each other until it's so late that the only dinner they can find is something deep-fried, meant for people who are very drunk at this stage of their evening. Marian calls this "fuck-fest dinner," delighting the boy with her use of profanity. He never swears, but giggles every time she does. She feels this could be dangerous for her vocabulary.

They talk a lot. They laugh together. They sleep entangled. Marian goes to work in a fresh shirt she has taken to carrying in her briefcase; Dan goes to his lectures at King's. She feigns alertness until she can see him again.

Can this be called "making love," she wonders, when no words of love are exchanged? No other term or description fits, no matter how she tries to make her mind flow around the word she won't allow herself to say. They have sex, yes, and you could certainly say that they fuck, the urgency and impatience not smoothed away by frequent meetings. Underneath it all, there is so much tenderness, so much of the unnamed, unknowable feeling. The other's pleasure is the ultimate reward for each of them; they compete to bring each other to the brink. Out of bed, they race to make each other tea, to give comforts, to spoil the other with small kindnesses. Still, neither of them will say the words.

A few times Marian's mouth is shaped around *I love you,* waiting only for her to breathe the sound into her confession.

Yet the words won't fall from her lips. She can tell, she can feel with her skin that she will spook him. This may be a whisper of her insecurity or an odd sense of empathy, but she fears that if she pulls away the drapery that covers up the intensity of her feelings, he will withdraw from her. She has done this herself to past lovers, when they got too involved for her comfort; she had felt that pulling away was the right thing to do, a kind thing to do. Now she pictures Dan taking a step back from her, and the imaginary pain makes her burst into tears on the train to work. She spends the day restless, listless. She feels better only when his arms are around her again, and he murmurs, "Coming back to mine tonight?"

They make love. She can't bear to think of it any other way. The boy is playful; he spells out words on her clit with his tongue and demands that she guess what he's writing. It's an impossible task, and she can't keep her mind on it anyway as pleasure wells up in her deep from her center.

"Enough of this!" she demands petulantly as she clutches his hair and tries to push his face down, into her. "Do your job, damn it."

"As milady commands!" he blurts, and proceeds to apply himself properly. The caresses of his tongue grow insistent; he knows her body now, knows its pleasure. Marian bites on a moan. Her fingers slacken in his hair, but when he whimpers, she knows it for disappointment, and grasps firmly again, gives his hair a good yank. He cries out, a long "Aah," of delight, and yet he fights to concentrate on bathing her clit with his lips and tongue.

As Marian crests the wave toward her climax, she realizes she has discovered the boy's secret.

She's too excited to bask in the glow of her pleasure and instead pulls on Dan's hair until he follows the unspoken instruction to come up for a kiss. She invades his mouth with her tongue, explores it thoroughly, leaving no illusion as to who has taken charge. He moans into her mouth, she can feel his stiffness against her thigh. She nibbles on his lower lip and, encouraged by the mewls of pleasure, gives it a solid bite; the boy cries out, but she can see his eyes roll back in enjoyment.

Holding his head steady by the hair, she pulls away and searches his face for clues that she may have guessed wrong. Dan is flushed; his eyes are unfocused with desire.

"So," she says softly, and adds a guess: "Boy."

"Yes, milady?" he breathes.

"Would you like me to hurt you?"

He averts his eyes, swallows hard. "Please," he says. And adds: "If you like?"

Her fingers stroke his blushing cheek. "I would like that very much." Her heart clenches with tenderness as she drinks in his vulnerable honesty.

She doesn't know much about giving pain beyond what she has seen or read by chance, but she believes in careful experimentation; with this in mind, she pushes Dan onto his back, slides on top of him and sinks her teeth into his shoulder. He yells, but keeps perfectly still. His cock is trapped between their bodies; she revels in how hard he has grown. She unclenches her teeth and carefully licks the bitten spot; the boy relaxes a little, but it's not long before her teeth have found a new target, eliciting a moan of pain. She leaves a trail of tooth marks down his arms, across his chest; makes him scream as her teeth close on his nipples.

"Good boy," she murmurs between bites, and reaches down to give his cock a little squeeze. Dan bucks his hips, thrusting into her hand. She laughs. "Ooh. Somebody is excited."

"Please," he pants. "Please, milady."

"Please, what?"

"Will you fuck me?"

"I might." Of course she will, but not before she draws her fingernails along his shaft, sinks them into the soft flesh, makes him writhe. They will need to talk about this; quite soon she will run out of guesses and will need better ideas of what turns him on, but for now this will do. The boy is whimpering, wriggling, unsure whether to thrust into her hands or to pull away from her nails; each of his frantic motions is a discovery, a new world for her to explore.

"Please, milady. Oh, please."

"Very well, then," she relents, now desperately hungry for him inside her. She mounts him in one swift thrust and leans forward to press both of his wrists into the pillow. His eyes are wide open, brimming with naked lust. He starts thrusting his hips up in the familiar frantic rhythm of their usual coupling.

Marian shoves her hips down, grinding her clit against his pelvic bone, and falls forward to fasten her teeth on his shoulder. His scream in her ear eggs her on, and she rides him to her climax without slackening the grip of her jaws, her fingers clenched tight around his wrists. As the boy comes, he chants her name between huge gulps of air, and she finally relaxes her jaws and lets go of his hands as they both rock together toward their silence.

They lie in each other's arms, glued together with cooling sweat. Dan's breathing is shallow, shaky.

He's the first to speak. "I'm not a freak."

She holds him tight. "Oh, sweetheart. Of course not."

"I know this. Honestly, I do. But many other people just... don't."

"Well, fuck them," says Marian.

Dan begins to laugh, and he laughs until he's crying, crying for a long time, face hidden in the hollow of her neck.

Marian strokes his back and waits for the storm to blow away on the wind, and her chest swells with tenderness.

With the tip of her finger she writes on his naked shoulder: *I L-O-V-E Y-O-U*. Her heart whispers the invisible words.

One day he will know her secret. One day her secret place will be open to him, like his is to her. One day. But not yet.

LOSER

Charlotte Stein

I don't know how I find myself here again, but somehow I always do. The same plasticky four walls of his scruffy trailer home. The same cranked-open cans of half-eaten beans lining the sideboard, the same evidence of the previous night's debauchery all over him like the reek of cheap booze that's right here, too. Everything not sexy and not cool.

Except for him.

Of course, rationally I know I shouldn't find him so. There's nothing cool about Loserville, and even if there was, you'd only have to look at him to know he's no good. He has a straggling, handlebar moustache crawling across his face like something a child scribbled. He sometimes gets caught wandering around town in nothing but his woolen long johns, stumbling and drunk and cussing everybody out. People call him Billy One-Strike, 'cause he's never met a woman who didn't like saying no to him.

Or a bank or a job or anything that didn't like to say no.

Except for me. I can't stop saying yes. The minute I realized

—with a little jolting start like a hiccup in my head—that he was coming on to me, something in me went away. I think the thing that went away is called dignity or pride or something like it, because that's what I'm missing as I stand before him, on a carpet that peels away from his walls like they're on fire.

Everything peels in here. Everything is insubstantial and about to fly away. There are cracks between the windows and the walls, cracks where the door doesn't fit its hole and the sharp winter air comes whistling in. There are cracks in me as he looks at me long and hard, with those dark, searing eyes.

They sparkle with knowing, those eyes. Even though he's got a can of chili in one hand and a falling-apart cigarette in the other, those eyes tell me why I'm here.

Because I can't stay away, I can't stay away, I wish I could, but dear god, I can't.

I tried to tell myself it was an accident, that first time; maybe I'd been drinking, even though I hadn't. Maybe I just liked how surprised he'd looked, when he said, *How about a drink, Mallory,* and I didn't immediately shoot him down. Maybe I had just been surprised that he knew my name and thought I was worth going for—unlike everyone else in this town. They call me Millie or Mindy or something else starting with *M,* whereas he had known it right off, no prompting.

He still knew it later on, when I fucked him up against the brick behind Hennessey's.

And of course I had known. I'd known that the dark alleyway with the bins and the tufts of snow at each corner—that's where he probably usually does it. If a girl's stupid enough to go with him, I bet he always takes her behind Hennessey's. Always drops to his knees and runs her skirt all the way up. Always kisses her between her legs in the same way other men kiss a girl's lips.

I didn't tell him. That no one else had ever done that before,

I mean. I didn't tell him. Instead I'd just wished I wasn't wearing woolen panty hose, so he could get to me faster, sooner, more. He did it sloppily and I could feel his moustache, but none of that's what I remember.

I remember how hungry he was, instead. How greedy. Like a man starved of human contact and just dying for his last meal. He had put his hands on my thighs and spread them almost roughly, then licked the length of my slit with the firm point of his tongue. Just like that. No waiting. Right on my clit, over and over, until I wanted to say some mysterious words like *thank you, thank you*.

Not that I actually did. I think fucking him was thanks enough. He seemed to think it a nice thank-you, when I pinned him to the brick and rutted up against him like something was wrong inside. That's what I am. Wrong inside.

I think he knows it, when he looks at me. He rarely says anything when I find myself in his trailer at three a.m., but it's not like I'm going to be here to share heartwarming tales of magic and wonder. I don't have a driveway I need plowing.

Or I do, but you know—in the metaphorical sense.

"You wanna drink?" he says, but I think he only ever does so because I always say no. It sharpens him, my no. It makes his shoulders go back. Behind him I can see the bed—it's a fold-out, and when it's down it takes up half his trailer—and it's obvious he's put on clean sheets, arranged the pillows just so.

The urge to leave rises up in me, like bile. But then he takes a step forward and kisses me just under the line of my jaw—in a place I didn't even know I liked—and I can't go anywhere. My eyes close of their own accord. I drift toward the press of his slippery mouth, without really wanting to.

It's kind of like falling asleep. You just drift, and the next thing you know you're dreaming about faraway worlds and wonderful things you never get to do, back in reality. Reality is people calling me Millie or Mandy or Maude.

This is something else. I don't know what this is. He's put the things in his hands down, and now they're full up with great bunches of my hair. I should really think about how nicotine- and food-stained his fingers are bound to be, but in truth he's really clean all over and even if he wasn't, I don't think I'd care.

I just want him to carry on insinuating his mouth against my frozen skin. It feels so hot I can hardly stand it, even though he should be freezing, too. He should be ice-cold and on the verge of death, the way winter's creeping in here.

But he isn't. I can feel the heat radiating off him until I'm faint with it, and then he just reaches down like he's dropped something on the floor, and gets underneath my dress. Just like that, with his mouth still on my throat!

One hand inside my panties, stroking and stroking.

He doesn't go about it slowly or fussily. There's no waiting for permission—though I suppose we're long past that, now. He knows what I need, and what I need happens to be his two fingers making a V along the length of my swelling, already-wet sex. He pushes down and his fingers glide, and then he pushes inward and sinks in to the hilt.

It really takes nothing at all. His other hand goes to my ass to steady me. His mouth stays scalding-hot and reassuring, at the curve where my throat meets my shoulder. And all of this happens while he fingers me, firmly, in and out like a piston until my legs start to tremble.

Of course I try to keep them under control. I try to keep all of me under control. But it's hard when his thumb has squirmed and sought out my clit, and he's rubbing it in sure circles while he fucks me and fucks me.

I clasp the back of his head when I come. His hair is very

fine, but there's absolutely loads of it, just masses of it, all shiny like varnished wood. I get a handful and hold on for dear life. It feels lovely—so silky—and it grounds me as I shake and shake and try not to shout loud enough for the neighbors he doesn't have to hear.

He lives out in the woods. No one's going to hear anything. Except for him, of course. He'll hear.

He waits for a long moment before he pulls away. And I feel his hand rub up and down my back, too, as though he's reassuring me first. When his fingers slide out of me, they do so slow and easy and he clasps my sex once, weird and firm, before he leaves the area entirely.

Then he just straightens up and looks at me with those sparkling eyes, all knowing and smug, most probably—only not, somehow. Now he looks at me with a strange sort of warmth, and when he speaks his voice is low and conspiratorial. Like maybe he knows I need some sort of quiet, some sort of hush.

"That what you needed, huh, baby?" he asks, and again I have this instinct to think the worst of him. To imagine smugness where there is none.

But I just can't imagine something out of nothing. His tone is lovely and inviting. He sounds pleased in a way I've never heard any other man sound pleased, and I can tell he's not trying to be cruel.

It's just a small, spare fact, like a part of myself I'd forgotten.

"Yeah," I say, and mean it.

Only then do I go to kiss him. I go to kiss him, but he interrupts me.

"You can go now, if you want. I won't hold it against you."

Something in me stops cold. Worse than before, when I saw his neatly made bed and the pillows and all the things he'd arranged, just for me. Does he mean it? I think he actually means it—that I could just come here and get off and then go, without giving him anything in return. And I can see it in his face—he doesn't mean it in the bad way. The bad, jeering way, as though I'm just this horrible girl who uses him and oh, I bet you're going to leave now, aren't you?

You selfish bitch.

But there's no selfish bitch written anywhere on his expression. There's just a frank pleasure over what he's just done to me, a satisfaction I've never seen anyone else have. I think he actually likes the idea that he can just get me off so easily. He revels in it in a way I've never seen him revel in a clean driveway or any of the other jobs he's failed so spectacularly at.

This job? This job he could *never* fail at. He's awesome at it. He's the best. I don't even get a little head hiccup, on realizing that. All those girls turned him down, and he's probably a better lover than any of their preppy Brads or Chads or Daves.

He does little things, like when I stop him saying words like those with my mouth on his, he brings his hands up to cup my face. Other guys don't cup my face. And he does it as though he wants to keep me as close as possible, so he can fully concentrate on my mouth and the way it moves and how much tongue I'm giving him at any given time.

He gives me good tongue right back. Never forceful, always urgent, just licking and licking into me the way he licks at my pussy, and oh, his lips are like...I don't even know. Flexible, very flexible.

And then there's the faint burn of his moustache, and his hands suddenly on my ass, stroking up my back, stroking all around and everywhere. His hands roam, shortly before we blunder into the bed and end up sprawled.

I think he knows I want him inside me. Usually I get to come, and then he fucks me. It's the order of things, the pattern we've fallen into—only this time I don't want that pattern. I want him to know something and know it hard, and I think I can show him this something with my mouth.

In fact I know I can, because when I strip those stupid woolen things off him and slide down his body, he makes a funny sound and then says:

"Oh, no, you don't have to..."

So I know it means something. It's different from the exchanges we've had before now. I'm going to take him in my mouth and suck him until he comes, and he's going to love it. He already loves it. When I just lick the slick, straining tip of his cock, his head goes back and he moans, long and loud—abandoned, in a way I wasn't.

And he gets louder, the more I dare to do. I start with just the firm, fat head of it in my mouth, sucking strongly until he bucks. Then I sink down, all the way to the base—he's big, but not so big that I can't manage a little deep-throating. It's the one thing I've had some real practice in—all those college boys who wanted nothing but.

However, they didn't talk the way he talks. If there's one thing that keeps me coming back for more, it's his dirty mouth. How it thrills through me, when he says such delicious naughty things with so much openness! All these *fucks* and *yeahs* and *So slippery, so tight, so hot, yes, yes, come on my cock, baby, that's it.*

I think I liked that last one, best of all. The way he pushes and cajoles me into orgasm, working me slow and easy, then fast and hard. He does the same thing here only without the vital physical component I'd need to actually come—though god knows my pussy clenches and pleasure flows through my body in thick waves, to hear him speak.

I think I know now how he makes me come so easily when we're fucking.

"Yeah, that's it, yeah—suck me. Oh, you're so good to me. Good girl...*Jesus.*"

He almost makes me come with his cock in my mouth. Just the words, god, just the words, in that wavering, twisted accent of his. And then the feel of him trying not to thrust and clutching at the back of my dress, cock swelling, the taste of precome on my tongue.

Everything is good and horny and right, and man, I'm dying to touch myself. I need it again, only moments after getting it so good I went weak, which is embarrassing—of course it is—but he's so awesome he knows how to make it okay.

He just touches me, without me having to ask. I'm on all fours with my ass in the air in a way that should probably be mortifying, but somehow it isn't when he slides a casual hand up my thigh and finds my cream-drenched slit.

He doesn't even have to work at it, really. I'm so wet he just glides right in without asking, spearing me with two fingers, like before, then switching things up just as I'm prepared for that. I think he's going for another slide in, only he veers right when he should have gone left and winds up with those same two fingers over my clit.

Of course I squirm. It's too much. Everything is too much. He's saying: "Is this what you want, baby, huh? You want some too—yeah, you want some. Fuck, look how wet you are, baby— is it making you wet, sucking me off like this?" And I'm going nuts. I suck him hard and sloppy and frantic, missing vital parts sometimes and hitting them dead on at others, my hand on him making up for all the stuff I can't easily reach.

"Yeah," he tells me. "Yeah, just like that, just that hard, do it hard, baby, hard."

His fingers trace small, faint circles over my bursting clit.

I don't know how he manages to stay so in control. I'm lost

before my second orgasm even starts to peak, toes curling, free hand clawing at him, all the thoughts of everything we've done swirling around inside my silly head.

I'm facing away from him, so I can't see what his face looks like when his hips jerk and his thighs tremble and he tells me he's coming, he's coming, but I remember the exact expression he gets, anyway. His mouth always comes open and his eyes roll back in his head, and the sounds that break out of him are like music, they are.

The taste of him is almost as good as those sounds. It's sharp, like the tang of his cheap aftershave or the bitter bleak thread of those horrid cigarettes he smokes—but it's good, too. All those thick spurts filling my mouth, as I watch his thighs drop to the mattress and his hand loosens its grip on the back of my dress.

I understand how he feels, even without the second orgasm. It's like a wound moving from sting to that sweet, aching burn. Everything relaxes and breaks down, and then we're just lying on the bed, panting, not speaking.

I guess maybe we don't have to speak. Words would only complicate things, anyway, at this point. If I used words, I'd have to ask him how come he lives like this, when it's obvious he could be something else, something better. And then he'd have to ask me what better is, exactly, and I don't know if I'd have an answer for that.

Better is my life, technically, but my life is watching shitty sitcoms in my pajamas, eating meals for one and falling asleep before I've even worked up the wherewithal to masturbate. Something about that doesn't seem better, exactly, and especially not when I'm sprawled on his threadbare mattress, with this low hum between my legs and the taste of his come still in my mouth.

It's almost funny when he says, "You still awake?"

Because in truth I'm not sure I've ever been more awake than

I am right now. Who knew that seediness and come in your mouth and someone's hand on your still damp thigh could keep you conscious? But it does.

"Yeah," I say, then repeat the word because once doesn't seem like enough. He should really know it a million times, and with those other words alongside it, too. Words like: you keep me conscious. Words like: you keep me afloat.

"You want me to give you another go around?" he asks, but this time I say no. I need to, because I'm working up to something else, instead. I think about it every time I'm in here, staring at his threadbare walls and his threadbare existence and all of the cold coming in so fierce you can see it in the air.

It's just a necessity, really. I mean—what if he died? What if he died, suddenly, of hypothermia? I'd be a terrible Samaritan, if I let a thing like that happen.

"Hey Billy," I say, and the words come out far less light and casual and good Samaritan-like than I intend. "You know, maybe next time you could come by my place."

In fact, I don't think that's good Samaritan-like at all. It just sounds like I'm asking him to come to my place and sleep in my bedroom, and when we wake up we can make eggs together and watch breakfast-time news. Then he'll go off and plow driveways, and I'll go off to the library, and when people say, *Hey, did I see Billy One-Strike coming out of your place this morning?* I'll say yeah.

Yeah, you did. He's my boyfriend. I think he's my boyfriend. Oh, dear god, I've used him so much that I don't even know if he'd ever want to be my boyfriend at all.

Until he says, "I love you, Mallory," right out of the blue. And then I guess I know.

HERE IN BETWEEN

Kristina Wright

*F*wapa-fwapa-fwapa.

The sound of a flat tire is so distinctive—and so pervasive in the confines of a small car—that it leaves a sickening, sinking feeling in your stomach, as if the tire isn't the only thing that has gone flat.

Getting a flat tire is bad enough. Having it happen at eleven o'clock at night on a desolate stretch of Tennessee highway is the worst kind of luck. Throw in the fact that I have no spare tire because I took it out to make room for my suitcase and no cell phone coverage because my service sucks outside of major cities, and I am smack dab in the middle of my worst nightmare.

I pull to the shoulder, the three good tires throwing gravel into the darkness. Shutting off the engine, I slam both palms on the steering wheel and curse the tire, the car and myself. The idea of hiking to civilization in the darkness is only slightly less appealing than waiting for dawn on the side of the highway.

I roll down the window to listen for traffic sounds and hear nothing but crickets and cows.

"Damn, damn, damn it to hell," I mutter, having run out of steam just as surely as my tire is out of air.

With nothing else to do, I get out of the car to examine the tire. Then, underestimating just how dark it is, I get back in the car to dig around in the glove box for a flashlight. I don't have a cell phone that works or a fourth tire or a spare tire, but I do have a reliable flashlight.

I am standing on the edge of the road, examining my faulty tire with its shiny new jewelry—a massive nail, judging by the size of the head—when a headlight comes over the ridge in the distance. At first, I think it is a motorcycle, but the silhouette of a pickup truck follows behind that single beam of light. The truck slows to a stop behind me and I have that momentary surge of feminine flight reflex. After all, who else would be on the road at this hour except a homicidal maniac?

I mentally talk myself down from my fear and stand my ground, even while I shift my grip on the Maglite from "flash-light" to "weapon of mass destruction." The creak of the pickup's door hints at a vehicle more decrepit than my twenty-year-old sports car, but the driver is anything but ancient. He saunters toward me as if he has all the time in the world to play hero to my damsel in distress, his lean body and tousled, longish dark hair silhouetted by that one headlight.

"Need help?" His accent isn't Tennessee twang, it's pure New York. Leave it to fate to send me a guardian angel from the very place I'm heading.

"Yeah. Got a spare tire for a 1990 Miata in the back of your truck?" Sarcasm is my fallback position when I'm tired or scared. And stranded, in this case.

His deep laugh is older than his face, but younger than his truck. "No, but I can give you a ride."

"Where am I?"

He runs a hand through his hair, which only serves to muss it more, and cocks his head to the side. In this light, his eyes look as black as his hair. "Well, you're sixty miles outside Nashville, but there's a motel about ten miles up the road that has the distinction of being across the highway from a decent garage. You can have them tow your car in the morning."

It seems so logical, so practical, and yet I am suspicious. "What are you doing out here?"

"Saving you from spending a night in what looks like a very uncomfortable car," he says.

He takes a couple of steps toward me. I contemplate whether to use my flashlight as a weapon when he leans down into my car and takes the keys from the ignition. He pops the trunk, grabs my suitcase and slams the trunk closed. Then he heads back the way he came as if he expects me to follow.

I once had a boss who wrote in my evaluation that I always meet or exceed expectations. My former boss was right. I am closing the passenger door on the truck only moments after he tosses my bag into the bed of the pickup.

"Thanks," I manage to say when he joins me in the truck, forcing the solitary word past a wall of exhaustion and frustration.

He drives with one hand on the steering wheel and the other arm propped out his open window. The smell of manure and fresh-cut hay fills the truck. It's not a bad smell when you're moving.

"Where you headed?" he asks, as we leave my sad little car behind.

"Manhattan."

His laugh is a bitter chuckle. "Go back the way you came. No good can come of it."

"No good could come from staying in San Diego, either," I mutter under my breath.

"Bad marriage, bad boyfriend or bad job?"

I debate answering him. Then I wonder why it matters what he knows. "All three. A lousy marriage led to a messy affair with my boss, who fired me to save his own ass."

My knight in shining armor has the balls to laugh at me. "Damn, lady. You're a whirling dervish of trouble."

If only he knew. But he doesn't need to know. "What about you? You're not from 'round these here parts," I say, putting on my best country accent.

He shrugs, easy like. "New York is where I'm from, but this is as good a place as any."

I raise an eyebrow in skepticism, but there is no way he can see my expression in the darkness. "If you say so."

We're quiet for the next few miles, and it's a comfortable silence. He pulls off the highway and into the motel parking lot. It's the kind of motel that is most often featured in horror movies, a single story of ugly cinderblock facing the highway, windows draped in bland, faded curtains. The vacancy sign flashes monotonously, the *n* burned out. There's a little tavern next door, close enough to walk to and stumble from.

I give an involuntary shudder. "How far did you say it was to Nashville?" He laughs, but he's already out of the truck and getting my suitcase. I follow him up to the motel office, feeling like this isn't my life. This isn't me.

The motel manager is a big, balding guy, sweating in the summer heat. He's watching some cop drama on a battered old television sitting on the counter.

"Hey, Buck. The lady got a flat a few miles down the road and needs a room for the night."

Buck glances from the TV to me. He stares at me so hard that I feel like I'm doing something dirty, even though I know

I'm not. He makes some sound in his throat that suggests acqui-
escence and checks a ledger.

"Sev'ty-nine fi'ty, plus tax," he grunts, his eyes squinting up
like he's staring into the sun.

"Buck," my savior says in a coaxing tone that borders on a
warning.

"Aw, Buddy, a man's gotta make a livin'."

I don't know if Buddy is my savior's given name or a nickname, but I watch them stare at each other. Then the sweaty
manager gives me the once-over and it's my turn to stare him
down.

He nods. "Fine, fine. Fi'ty bucks."

I fork over my credit card and we wait while Buck runs it.
He hands over a plastic tag with a key attached—the first real
key I've seen for a hotel room in at least a decade—and he jerks
his thumb behind him. "Room's 'round back. Ice machine on
the end."

Outside, I say, "I would have paid double just to get out of
there."

"The room's worth half what you paid."

I open the door to the room and fumble for the light switch
by the door, expecting the worst. I'm pleasantly surprised. It's
not exactly the Four Seasons, but at least it's clean. There's
a double bed with a hideously ugly floral print bedspread, a
couple of battered end tables and a matching dresser with a
slightly bigger television than the one in the motel office that
predates remote controls. At the opposite end of the room is the
door to the bathroom. I figure it can't be worse than the room
and if it's clean, I'll survive.

He's standing behind me in the doorway, as if not sure what
to do.

"Thanks. Nice of you." I sit on the edge of the bed. I've hit a wall of exhaustion so big and wide I can't even form proper sentences. Realizing I sound like Buck, grunting words instead of speaking sentences, I force a smile. "I mean, you really didn't have to stop for me. So, thank you. I appreciate it."

His smile transforms his face from merely good looking to almost stunning. I catch my breath and slap my hand over my mouth, pretending it's a yawn. The twinkle in his eyes tells me he knows better.

"You're welcome."

Without invitation, he crosses the room to stand beside me. For a minute, I think he's going to kiss me. Which is silly, because we've spent all of thirty minutes together and I don't even know his name.

He takes up the thin little pad of paper and generic ballpoint pen by the phone and jots something down. "I'll give Joe at the garage a call in the morning and let him know where your car is. Here's my number. Call me if you have any problems." He hesitates. "Or if you need anything."

He hands me the pad instead of putting it down on the table. I look up at him, not sure what to say. I go for simple. "I will. Thanks."

The door closes behind him with a quiet *snick*. It's been a long time since I stayed in a roadside motel. A long time since I've even been alone like this. It's strangely exhilarating.

I stretch out on the bed. It's not so bad. The springs creak a little, but the pillow is thick and downy and the mattress has a comfortable give to it. I'm still holding the pad of paper with his number. I hold it up and look at it: just his number, no name. Like he's mine and I can call him whatever I want.

I close my eyes and think about that for a minute. Then I open my eyes and reach for the phone. I'm put off for a moment because it's an old rotary-style phone. Then I laugh.

It's perfect. Just like everything else about this night, all the parts fitting together into some puzzle. Only a few key pieces are still missing and I can't quite make out yet what the picture is supposed to be.

He answers on the first ring, as if he expected me to call. "Yeah?"

"Can you come back?"

"Be there in five minutes." He doesn't ask why and I like that. Simple. Easy.

I leave the door cracked open for him while I get in the shower. Maybe it's not a good idea, inviting him back or leaving the door open, but driving cross-country in a twenty-year-old car hadn't been a good idea, either. My whole life to this point feels like a long list of bad ideas. So what's a couple more in a string of them?

I take my time in the shower, knowing he won't join me. I don't know why I know that, I just do. He'll respect my privacy because he's a private kind of guy. Yeah, I'm sure of it.

When I come out, warm and wet and wrapped in my own robe and wearing my own fuzzy socks because cheap motels don't offer things like robes and slippers, he's sitting on the bed. There's a bottle of whiskey—the good stuff—on the bedside table, along with two tumblers. I raise an eyebrow and look at him.

There's that shrug again, like he's letting everything slide right off his shoulders. "I was going to see if you wanted to go next door for a drink. When I heard you in the shower, I figured you'd rather stay in."

I nod and sit down on the other side of the bed. His shirt-sleeves are rolled up and the cuffs ride up when he reaches across the bed to hand me a glass. I have a weakness for forearms and his are tan and muscular. He pours me some whiskey—enough that it's a serious drink, not so much that I'm at risk of spilling it—then he pours his own. We sit there like that, me in a robe and him in well-worn jeans and a black shirt, like we're old friends who just ran into each other and decided to have a drink in the middle of a motel bed that sags on the side closest to the bathroom.

He stares at the blank television while I stare at his profile. He has a nice face, a kind face. I wonder what his name is, but I don't ask. I contemplate him and puzzle over it. He's from New York, so it's not some country name. They might call him Buddy down here in Tennessee, but his given name is something different, I decide. Something serious. Henry, maybe. Or Luke. Maxwell or Nathan, possibly.

I realize suddenly that he's watching me watch him. He smiles again, softly. Tiredly. There is a scar at the corner of his lip, only about half an inch long, but wide enough that it looks taut and silvery against his tan. It must have hurt, whatever cut deep enough to leave a scar like that. I want to lean over and kiss that flaw on an otherwise perfect mouth.

There's nothing stopping me; nothing but a few inches of bed and a glass of whiskey that's almost gone already.

He sees me coming and meets me halfway. Then he stops.

"This is one of those moments," he says, staring at my mouth. "Those in-between moments."

I think he must be drunk already. "What are you talking about?"

"You know, the time after one thing, but before another."

I consider what he means. "Like, for me, after I left San Diego, but before I arrive in New York."

He smiles big, nodding. His hair flops down over his fore- head, making him look rakish. "Yeah. You get it. We're here in between two things."

"I guess." I might understand what he means, but that doesn't mean I understand where he's going with it.

"This is a powerful moment," he says. "It's like the moment before your tire went flat. One minute you thought you knew your path, the next minute—" He waves his hand in the air as if clearing smoke. "Your whole path was changed."

"And if I kiss you?" I ask, because I really want to understand. "Does that put me on a new path?"

He contemplates my question, then nods. "Yeah, though you may not think so here in between before the kiss and after."

I laugh. "You act like it's a given I'm going to kiss you." His smile fades and he looks at me, his dark eyes heavy lidded. It could be sleep or lust. Lust, I think. Or maybe that's my own conceit talking.

"It is," he says. "It was a given the minute your tire went flat. That in-between moment led to this one. This one will lead to the next one."

"Et cetera," I say. Or try to say. All I manage is "Et" before his lips are on mine.

For two strangers who've known each other just a couple of hours and are already drinking whiskey in bed while one of them is mostly naked, it's a pretty tame kiss. His mouth is as soft as I expected it to be, except for his scar. It's a solid ridge of tissue beneath my lips. I tease it with my tongue, as if I could soften it.

We kiss slowly, leisurely, each of us still holding our glass. I'm on the side of the bed closest to the bathroom, sitting in that little gulley in the mattress, so that he's a little above me. I reach out with my free hand and wrap it around his wrist, the one that doesn't have a drink. I feel him shift away and I'm surprised to feel a sharp pang of disappointment. Did I really want to be kissing a stranger in a cheap motel? Did I really want more than that?

I don't have time to answer the questions because he's coming back, this time to take my glass away and put it with his on the table. Then he's wrapping his arms around me and pulling me down on the bed with him. But *pulling* isn't the right word—he's laying me down where I want to be, as if I had been frozen in place and not able to get there on my own.

I hold on to him, my hands on his bare forearms, feeling the flex of muscle as he props himself over me. His lips part and his tongue teases mine, tasting like the bottom of my whiskey glass, making me want more.

I slide my hands up to his shoulders, then around his back, pulling him down on top of me. I want to feel his weight, pressing me into the hollow of the mattress. I want him on top of me, inside me. His tongue is in my mouth or I would be begging him for more.

The belt on my robe isn't tied off tight—nothing about me is wrapped too tightly right now—and it doesn't take much for him to get it open, to get his hand between my legs. He's hard; I can feel his erection against my thigh. Of course he's hard; he had to be. He's hard because I'm wet—or is it that I'm wet because he's hard?

He slips a finger inside me and I'm not sure who breaks the silence first. He inhales sharply as I moan, as if he didn't expect me to be wet. I feel like a slut. I feel like a goddess. I just *feel*.

He kisses me as he plays with me, his hand angled between us in a way that must be uncomfortable for him, but he doesn't complain. He thumbs my clit and I feel everything inside me tighten. I'm trying to turn off my brain, to forget the last time I was with a man, to forget the men who have come before. There are only so many ways to fuck and after a while it's hard not to compare one experience to another, to not be thrown back in time to a different place, a different bed, a different man, when the one you're with touches you just so. But I'm trying. Dear god, I'm trying.

His thumb finds a rhythm, or maybe my body just matches the rhythm he sets, but whatever it is, I'm coming fast and quick, pleasure overriding memory, drowning out my surprise. He keeps his hand there, cupping my pussy, squeezing and stroking me as I come. I cling to his shoulders and ride his hand, gasping and moaning, but not moaning his name, because I don't know it.

Before I even have time to catch my breath, he's pulling away, leaving me. I say something incoherent, maybe I even yell it, something to let him know I don't want him to leave me. He's mumbling something about a condom, fumbling around in his jeans pocket, the jeans halfway down his lean hips, his cock jutting out thick and heavy from between his thighs.

I want to tell him I don't give a damn about safe sex, because I don't right here, right now. I will later, I'll care a lot, but right now I just want him inside me.

"There," he says, sliding the condom on, his jeans around his knees now.

I want to laugh at the incongruity of it—that he'd take the time to put on a condom but not to take off his jeans. But then he's inside me and the thought flutters away with the condom wrapper.

I expect him to be quick, to fuck me hard, but he's full of surprises. He starts slow, letting me get used to him. He goes from stranger to lover in the span of a heartbeat, my body seeming to know just how he will move and matching him stroke for stroke. I'm holding his hips, stroking his ass, feeling the rough fabric of his jeans against my lower legs, the dampness of the robe beneath me.

The old bed creaks beneath us, a friendly, welcoming sound.

It's known a lot of lovers, but it's never known us. I trail my hands up his back, soothing the muscles as I go, and then tangle my fingers in his hair. It's thick and curly at the nape of his neck and I hold on tight as he dips his head to my breasts and trails kisses over them. His lips find my nipple, suckle it gently, then move to the other one. I'm whimpering low in my throat, almost a keening sound; I want him so much.

I tug him up by his hair until he's looking into my eyes. Then I pull his head down so I can kiss him again. He stares into my eyes until the split second before our mouths meet and then his eyelids drop, long, dark lashes casting beautiful shadows on his cheeks. This is a kiss of lovers, and there is nothing tame about it. It drives him deeper into me, makes him slip his hands under my ass and pull me up to meet his thrusts. It's the kiss that makes him fuck me harder, faster, rougher. And I love it like that, so I keep kissing him, keep my fingers in his hair, keep my legs wrapped around his back even though it feels like I'm going to split in two from the sweet agony of his cock inside me. He's moaning into my mouth and I'm swallowing his voice, taking every part of him that he'll give me.

Then I'm coming again, the sensation almost painful it's so strong. I scream and hear my voice—unfamiliar, like a thousand other voices before me in this room. He's gone still against me and I know he's coming, too. I keep rocking against him, tightening around him, wanting him to feel as good as he's made me feel.

Time stops in that moment. It's that in-between moment he was talking about, between the before and the after. I want to stay there, forever. I can't, I know I can't. But I want to.

His weight is a comfort, though I know it won't seem that way for long. I can feel his heart racing against my chest, matching the throb of his cock inside me. He groans as he shifts off me,

I groan from the emptiness he leaves behind. Side by side, we contemplate the ceiling.

I'm the one to break the silence. "So, what's your story?"

"What's *your* story?"

I close my eyes. If you've seen one dingy motel ceiling, you've seen them all. "I already told you my story."

He laughs, a satisfied, masculine laugh. It's different from his laugh earlier, as if I've given him something, filled up some part of him. "Oh, sweetheart, you haven't told me your story. You've only told me the last chapter."

I like that. "Fine. Tell me *your* last chapter. Are you a poet or philosopher? You sound like both."

"Something like that. I write music. Play, too." His words are starting to blur, more likely from sleep than that one whiskey we had.

"Anything I might have heard?"

He shrugs, his shoulder rising and falling against mine. "Maybe. Probably."

"So you're not chapters, you're songs," I say, pleased with the analogy. I like his warmth and I curl on my side to get closer to it, inhaling his scent.

"Baby, I'm a whole lot of songs."

"Maybe you'll play me another one," I whisper, trying to make it a come-on, but feeling that slow, steady pull of sleep now that my eyes are closed. I want more of him, but I don't have the energy to make it happen.

He slips his arm around me and pulls me in tight against the hollow of his shoulder. Then he kisses my forehead so tenderly I feel the hot sting of tears behind my eyelids. Whiskey always makes me a sentimental fool, I tell myself, not entirely believing my own lie.

"I'll sing every one," he promises. His lie, I believe.

* * *

I wake up disoriented and frantic. It takes me a minute to recognize the room, to remember where I am and what happened. I can smell him on my skin, but he's gone. He tucked me in before he left, though, and I pull the sheet up to my nose and inhale him. Us.

Sunlight is streaming through a crack in the faded curtains, but I'm in no rush to get up. I yawn and stretch, feeling the pleasant heaviness between my legs that reminds me of him all over again. I push away any emotions that threaten to bubble to the surface. I focus on the tasks at hand: take a shower and get dressed, get my car from the garage, get on the highway going east, get to New York—if not today, then tomorrow.

It's a good plan and it propels me up and out of bed and into the shower. I hope he's called the garage like he said he would. For some reason, I'm sure he has.

The water feels good on my body, soothing my road-weary muscles and all those other places that were well used the night before. I'm not sorry I slept with a stranger—I'm only sorry he didn't stick around this morning for more.

I never unpacked the night before, so I get dressed out of my suitcase. My hair is still damp and I'm not wearing makeup, but it doesn't seem to matter. The guys at the garage won't care what I look like as long as my credit card is good and I'll be on the road all day, anyway. With one last wistful glace at the rumpled bed, I open the door.

And there he is, standing in the parking lot next to his truck. My car is on a little flatbed trailer hitched to his truck, the tire still flat. It's early and I haven't had any coffee yet, so it takes me a minute to say anything. In the meantime, I look from him to my car, back to him.

"The garage doesn't have a tire for your car and can't get it for a week."

"So you're going to drive me to Nashville?" I ask as he takes my suitcase.

He throws it in the back of the truck and opens the passenger door for me. Once I'm inside and he's closed the door, he grins at me through the open window. "Something like that."

I have to wait for him to walk around the truck and climb in before I can ask, "Something like that? So where are you taking me?"

He starts the engine and eases out onto the highway, my little old red car behind his faded old red pickup. He gives me another crooked grin, almost shy this time. "I was thinking I'd take you on into New York."

He says it like New York is closer than Nashville. I blink, then nod. Why the hell not?

"You're going to take me to New York." It's a statement, not a question, but he nods along with me.

"So what happens now?" I ask. "What happens here in between?"

He accelerates until the wind is whipping through the truck, flinging my long hair this way and that. The sun is over a ridge in the distance and we're heading for it.

"I sing you my songs," he says. "And you tell me if you've heard them before."

He does.

And I have.

SPELLBOUND

Garnell Wallace

My name is Kia Monet and my family thinks that I'm under a voodoo spell. It is the only way for my Haitian-born parents to explain why I'm wasting my life in the slums of Port-au-Prince with a low-budget filmmaker instead of being a trust-fund trophy wife in California.

If I was under a spell, it was Jonah's smile, Jonah's voice reciting French poetry in the dark during a respite from his magnificent cock. His cock *is* black magic; an evil one-eyed sorcerer, powerful enough to turn me into a quivering mass of nerves with just one twitch. I like to sleep with it buried deep inside me, its comforting pliability lulling me into the blissfulness of sleep. Even his long, tapered fingers buried deep in my pussy can bring on multiple experiences of what we French call *la petite mort,* or the little death, when you are so inflamed with passion at the moment of surrender it feels like you are about to surrender your soul as well. I've died a thousand times in Jonah's arms in the time we've been together. With each rebirth,

I feel more alive, more like the person I am meant to be. I am bewitched and have no desire to be cured.

We met at his small film production studio in the midst of a dusty, vibrant, colorful mix of vendors, loud music, chatter and the general chaos of a dense Caribbean city. Before then, he'd been a name scribbled on a piece of paper, a possible contact for my documentary film profiling Haitian women. As we shook hands, I thought how he should be in front of the camera instead of behind it. He had a face made for pictures, with surprisingly Anglo features and a tall, muscular body, all wrapped in dark chocolate skin topped by waist-length dreadlocks. He was very different from the rich boys I'd dated in California. He had a take-it-or-fuck-it kind of attitude I found refreshing after a lifetime of keeping up appearances, and my mother's desperate attempts to strip away anything that could label me as an "immigrant." I looked like my father, with pale skin and light gray eyes. I could've passed for white, except for a defiant mop of kinky black hair I'd refused to let my mother straighten.

My parents felt that I'd romanticized Haiti. It's violent and raw, and yet there were people like Jonah, who saw beauty among the ashes and felt it was their duty to make a difference instead of running away. I've had to learn what it means to be a biracial woman in America, and fight against Jim Crow's one drop rule, but I'd never explored what it meant to be Haitian. I used to horde everything about Haiti that I could get my hands on: books tucked safely under my bed like cherished porno magazines, music in Creole and French. I'd learned about voodoo and the darker side of the Haitian culture. Like a moth to a flame, I'd risked my mother's disapproval for just a glimpse into what I felt was still a part of me.

This was my first time back to Haiti since I was three, but it immediately felt like home. I felt a sense of camaraderie with the women who graciously allowed me into their lives. We conversed in Creole; the broken French my mother despised rolled easily off my tongue.

From the moment I met Jolie, sitting like a regal queen in her luxurious bordello, I was a little intimidated by her. She proudly discussed how she started her business, then sat back and stared at me with beautiful catlike eyes.

"You will never know what it means to fully be a Haitian woman unless you can embrace your God-given sexuality," she said.

I felt as if my lens was suddenly turned toward me and I squirmed in my chair.

"I've seen the way you crave Jonah. He wants you but he won't make the first move. He's afraid of upsetting your delicate American sensibilities." She laughed softly. "When you live in a country where you have limited rights and opportunities, you take full advantage of the ones you do have."

But giving in to the lust I felt for Jonah wasn't so easy in the beginning. I convinced myself that I couldn't sleep with a man I'd just met. I wasn't that kind of girl. The first night, he invaded my dreams and I awoke in the midst of a fiery orgasm. I realized my hands were between my legs, massaging the slippery little nubbin of hard flesh that had seemed uncharacteristically greedy and demanding since my arrival on the island.

I got out of bed and stared at myself in front of the floor-length mirror across from my bed. Sweat had molded the T-shirt to the contours of my voluptuous chest. My nipples pointed straight out as if begging to be touched, and I reached out and pinched them. I pulled the T-shirt over my head and moved to the large French doors in a futile search for relief.

Across from my bedroom, Jonah's house was ablaze with

light. He seemed to work well into the night. I envisioned him toiling intently while beads of sweat dappled his smooth skin. I saw myself, pointed tongue licking up the salty drops. A part of me wanted to walk the short distance to his house and turn my fantasies into reality. A whiff of cool air danced around me, carrying a hint of night jasmine. The wind seemed to whisper, urging me to take a chance. It slithered between my legs, fueling the flames already building in my twitching pussy.

I shook my head. There was no way I could do it. Yet, even as I acknowledged this fact, my feet started moving, taking me in the direction of the unknown. I needed to do this, I conceded. I needed to just fuck him and get it over with. There was no way that the reality could be as electrifying as my dreams; it never was.

I was so focused on what I was about to do that it didn't register that I was boldly naked, walking up the front steps of the house of a man I'd known less than a week. The door was slightly ajar and without even thinking to knock, I pushed it open and walked into Jonah's studio.

As I'd imagined, Jonah was working at a long, low table. He wore only tight jeans, beads of sweat and a smile. He didn't seem in the least bit surprised to see me. Beginning at my pale mauve toenails, his eyes slowly slid up my body, taking in every inch while I stood there panting and building up my courage, and anger.

His confidence infuriated me. He was so sure of himself and the power he had over me. I'd been going to pieces since I'd met him and he'd been quietly biding his time knowing full well that I would be the one to break down first and come begging. I latched on to my anger; it boosted my courage and gave me the strength to walk over to him. He started to say something but I shook my head and placed my index finger over his lips.

I didn't want to talk, I didn't want foreplay; I didn't even want kisses. All I wanted was to get those damn tight jeans off of him and impale myself on his big, brown cock. He licked my finger and I pulled my hand away from his face and sank between his legs. With trembling fingers I slowly slid his zipper over the bulge in his pants. He lifted his hips and I pulled the jeans down to his ankles. I stared at his black boxer-briefs for a second, then took a deep breath and pulled them down. His cock sprang free like a fleshy boomerang. My intention was to jump on him and ride it like the devil himself was chasing me, but its sheer perfection held me spellbound.

I reached out and ran my fingers down its length. I'd expected it to be impressive in size and girth, but I hadn't expected a finely crafted tool wrapped in skin as smooth and luxurious as the best quality leather. The mushroom head resembled the work of a master craftsman and flowed seamlessly into a thick shaft and smooth testicles. His entire body deserved to be immortalized in fine marble like Michelangelo's *David*.

I felt I had to savor it, if only for a moment. If I didn't, I would forever regret not knowing if his cock tasted as good as it looked. This was my one chance. When I was done with him, I'd walk out of his house and it would be strictly business between us from then on.

I flicked my tongue out and sampled him with small curling licks. He tasted like the ocean; maybe he'd gone for a swim earlier to cool off, I surmised. Not that it'd done him any good. I fully intended to have him far beyond the boiling point before I left. Amongst the salt from the ocean and his sweat, I caught a hint of his own unique taste. Craving more, I enveloped him in the moist heat of my mouth. Spurred on by his loud moans and his painful tug on my hair, I used my tongue and teeth on every inch of him. I felt like I was drowning in the taste and feel of him and, fearing my courage would desert me before I could complete my mission, I reluctantly stood up and quickly straddled him, attempting in the same hurried manner to impale myself on him.

But the size of the tip cautioned me to take it slow. Bit by delicious bit, my pussy stretched to accommodate him. He was so hot I felt as if I was about to melt, but the sticky wetness I felt I was dissolving into was only there to ensure a fluid fuck as I began to frantically grind my hips against him.

Jonah seemed to understand that I didn't want him to touch me. Though my breasts and lips tingled for attention, I wanted the sweet ache to end—yet I could've bounced happily on his lap for the rest of the night.

Jonah slid lower until only his upper body remained in the chair. Now free to move his hips, he took the control away from me. Supporting himself with his strong legs, he grabbed my firm behind and surged up into me. A hot moan escaped my parched throat. He was so powerful, growling beneath me like a sleek jungle animal. My pussy was so slick yet there was enough friction between us for me to feel as if I was burning. One hand slipped between my cheeks, making me gasp as I felt a finger tentatively probe the puckered entrance. I went still and managed to croak out a soft no. I wasn't sure if he'd heard me but when I felt him push forward I couldn't muster up the strength to say it again.

He'd taken away my control and completely shocked me. I felt betrayed by my own body. Despite the taboo of what he was doing to me, the little bitch wanted more; made me beg for it, in fact. I broke my own rule about no talking and somehow became fluent in a vernacular that would've made the most seasoned sailor blush. Finally I ran out of energy and words and could only sob in ecstasy while he manipulated my body and bent it to his will.

It scared me that he had so much control over me. The reality of having him deep inside me was so much better than anything my limited imagination could ever have conjured up. The mad rush of emotions, feeling as if I needed him even more than my next breath; it was all more than I could've ever hoped for.

I grabbed the arms of the chair and gyrated my hips in an effort to gain back some of my control. Sweat poured from my body onto Jonah's face and unbelievably he opened his mouth and caught the sweat falling from my breasts like mother's milk. The sight of it severed the last fragile tethers of my control and my orgasm crashed around me like large waves from the nearby ocean. As I watched Jonah reach and go over the brink to his release, my insatiable body managed another rippling of waves. When I finally stopped shuddering and was sure my legs could support me, I got up and without looking at him, I bolted out the door.

The next morning he invited me over for coffee and I never left. We didn't discuss what was happening between us. I'm not sure I even knew. All I knew was that I couldn't resist him. At the end of each day, in Jonah's tiny apartment, we discussed my film. The entire apartment was just one room with a little attached bathroom. From a small kitchen tucked in one corner, Jonah fed me from the rich palette of Haitian cuisine. His bedroom led out onto a small balcony overlooking a farmers' market where we shopped for fresh produce every morning. Much of the small space was covered with books, music and DVDs. A local jazz band usually played in the background while we sipped lemonade from old glasses in a vain attempt at relief from the heat. It was unusually hot for January. I was more comfortable in his one-room house than I'd ever been in my parents' luxurious six-bedroom home, even though I couldn't seem to keep my eyes from straying to Jonah's naked, sweaty body beside me.

"It's better to work naked in this heat," he'd explained after stripping.

His cock, resting lazily in his lap, always made it very difficult for me to concentrate.

"Jolie is an amazing woman," I said, though I was looking at his cock when I said it. I forced my eyes to my computer screen. "She actually considers herself an entrepreneur and not just a madam. And by catering to a mostly foreign elite clientele, she's actually providing women with a safe environment and a chance to make a decent living and take care of their families."

"Do you admire or condemn her?" Jonah asked.

"I admire the courage it takes to live her life on her own terms. The women here are so strong. In America it seemed that I was given everything but a backbone."

Jonah reached over and caressed the side of my face. "What you're doing now takes courage. Never forget what an amazing woman you are." I didn't feel so amazing. I didn't even have the courage to closely examine my feelings for him. I was too afraid that if I tried to define it, if I pushed him into loving me, our little bubble would burst.

I grabbed his hand and kissed it. "You always know how to make me feel better." I slid his hand down my face and neck and placed it over one perky breast. His hand slipped into my lacy black bra and squeezed my nipple. I moaned, and the deep sound awakened his cock. It sprang to life like a cobra ready to pounce. I reached in back and unhooked my bra. My ample breasts spilled out of their confinement but already his hand was moving down to my sticky crotch. I opened my legs a little wider and Jonah slipped one finger in through the side. I stood up and pulled my wet panties off. His cock, now fully erect, beckoned me between his spread thighs.

"Turn on the camera," Jonah whispered before licking his finger.

I turned around and set up the camera lying next to my computer. Jonah loved to film us having sex. Before him, I'd thought sex was something you did in the dark, but he relished every minute. Under his tutelage, I've learned that sex is something to be celebrated, even when it is nasty and dirty. I liked it dirty; I liked feeling so hungry I wanted to devour his chocolate cock.

I moved to Jonah's side so the camera could fully capture me worshipping his cock. I dipped my tongue into his navel first, causing him to jump slightly. I then circled his navel and balls before positioning my mouth over his twitching rod. I wet the head first and then swallowed most of him in one hungry gulp. The taste of him—salty, earthy—flowed around me like a spell I hoped would never be broken. I would've gladly become his slave for the rest of my life to feel as freely as I did when I was with him. I didn't know if it had been love at first sight, but I told myself that I didn't need to define it, especially since I was just trying to define me. All I knew was that it felt good; my god, it felt good!

I felt Jonah tug on my hair, warning me that he couldn't take it any longer. I stood up and straddled him. I reached down between us and grabbed his cock and ecstatically impaled myself on it. I cried out, free to be loud and brazen. My cries mingled with the African drums on the stereo. I listened to the hypnotic rhythms that seemed to call from the Motherland, daring me to embrace the island girl in me. Jonah's fiery tongue licked my breasts as I started to move my hips in time to the music. I was an island girl then, dancing barefoot on my lover's lap, breasts and hips swaying to the beat of my own drums. I leaned forward so the camera could document the beauty of my body swallowing and releasing his cock. Jonah dug his fingers into my firm cheeks and spread them like a rare flower. Jonah's cries of release were loud and unabashedly primal. I came with a flood of tears. Afterward, I curled up in Jonah's arms, big, strong arms that made me feel safe despite the turmoil outside and the conflict in my heart.

On Sunday he made me breakfast with a hard-on: American-style bacon, sausages and eggs. When he served me, I reached out and fondled his sausage. He swatted my hand away. He called it tantric sex; I just saw it as frustrating. I watched him as he sipped strong black coffee and read the paper. I didn't see the point of desire that leads nowhere.

"It's about discipline and desire," Jonah explained without looking up. "You will never feel closer to a divine power."

"What power do you subscribe to?"

"I'm inclusive of all religions, but I was raised by my mother and grandmother, who are Voodoo priestesses."

I put my fork down. "So you know how to use black magic and cast spells on people?"

Jonah neatly folded his paper. "Tell you what—you get naked and we'll have a very insightful discussion about religion."

My parents had raised me to be a good Christian, though I was somewhere left of where they'd hoped I'd be. I don't think any religion has all the answers, and I don't think we're meant to have them. If we were all-knowing, why would we need a higher power? Anxious to hear Jonah's views, I pulled my T-shirt over my head and threw it on the floor. I felt naughty having my bare bottom on his plastic chair. A whiff of cool air caressed my bare skin and it was hard not to concentrate on the sensuality of being naked in the kitchen. In an effort not to, I repeated my question.

"Black magic is separate from Voodoo," Jonah explained. "Voodoo is a religion, much like Christianity or Buddhism.

Black magic is how people twist the religion to suit their own wicked desires. I'd never use it because it boomerangs. You Christians call it reaping what you sow, the Buddhists call it karma; I just call it stupid."

We spent the morning discussing religion and politics, philosophy and pop culture. Jonah had traveled the world; lived in South Africa, Japan and France. He spoke five languages and never wanted children. I too had no desire to procreate in a world gone mad.

"If Haiti becomes a better place in my lifetime, maybe I'll reconsider," he told me.

We walked around the apartment with our bodies longing to connect while we touched only with our hearts and minds. I watched sweat drip down his body and I envied it the pleasure of his skin. I itched to slide my hand up the crest of his ass, to linger at the small of his back and beg him to fuck me. But he ignored the persuasiveness in my eyes. After a while though, it did become easier to ignore the persistent throb between my thighs. By afternoon, my efforts were rewarded by warm touches and long, intimate kisses. But it was only under the cover of darkness, after he'd recited the last poem, that I was finally allowed to touch Jonah's cock, to marvel at its restraint and assert that no matter how long it took, I still had the power to make it lose all measure of self-control.

Time truly does fly when you're having fun. It seemed in no time I'd shot my last footage of Haiti, of the peaceful mountains and the turbulence of its cities. I'd said good-bye to people I considered my friends—the children playing in the streets, their sense of wonder still intact in the face of such abject poverty, the mothers who prayed for a better world for them to play in. They were all indelibly imprinted in my heart, as they were in my film.

I clung to Jonah, fully aware that in a few hours, I'd be on a plane, and I'd have to learn how to ignore my cravings for his kisses, for the feel of his smooth chest against my fingers, for the black magic between his legs luring me to kneel before it. I'd have to content myself with seeing it on film and in my dreams. I'd miss his wisdom, his poetry, and his tiny apartment with the unbearable heat that had become my oasis.

I pushed the future out of my mind and concentrated on his warm breath fanning my face. His hands dug into my ass and he lifted me and carried me to the bed. I asked for a poem while he undressed me and he recited one of his own: "It's called 'Kia's Eyes.' *I'm at peace looking into Kia's eyes; filled with pain and passion.*" He stared longingly at me. "*I'm going to miss looking into Kia's eyes.*"

His words surged over my breasts, plunged between my legs and incited a riot of pleasure throughout my body. I knew I'd carry his voice with me. On the days when I really miss him, I'll recall one of his poems, and I'll be back in Haiti again, feeling his dreadlocks caress my skin as he slithers down my body; a beguiling sorcerer weaving his spell on a most willing participant.

I woke up in Jonah's arms for the last time. I watched him sleep, memorizing features that were already etched in my memory forever.

He smiled. "It's not the last time we'll see each other," he said without opening his eyes.

I kissed his lids. "I know, I just like looking at you." My hand slipped down to his cock. "All of you."

"When will I see you again?" I asked. I trailed my fingers and my gaze down his chest to avoid looking directly into his beautiful eyes.

Jonah sighed. "I can't say right now; we're both sort of

married to our careers. But we'll find a way to make it work."

My fingers stilled. "Make what work? What exactly do we have here?"

"Isn't that what we're trying to figure out?"

I looked up at him. "If we don't know when we'll see each other again, doesn't that say we're defining us as nothing serious?"

Jonah sat up. "So what should I do to show you how much I care about you? Beg you to stay, to give up your life and help me fight the good fight? That's not a decision I want you to make just because you met me."

"I guess I just hoped you'd want me more." I got up and started dressing.

Jonah did the same. "You hoped I'd want you to give yourself permission to want me. That's not how it works, baby."

"You're right. We're not ready for anything serious."

Suddenly the room started to rumble. Instinctively I reached for Jonah and he pulled me to the ground. I heard the evidence of our lives crashing down around us. I heard people screaming outside and Jonah's voice telling me it would be okay. It seemed like ages before I felt his weight lift from me.

"Are you okay?" he asked, and I nodded yes.

"Stay here," he ordered.

I dared to open my eyes, then got up and examined the mess. Jonah was already out the door. I went after him but stopped at his gate where the earth had literally disappeared. All around there was chaos, like hell had opened up and poured its fury on the city, which looked like something out of an apocalyptic movie. Being from California, I knew what an earthquake felt like, but I'd never imagined anything could be so destructive and horrific. The minutes slipped into hours, which slipped into days, most of which passed in a blur. As soon as they could, my parents sent a plane to deliver aid and bring me home, but I refused to leave.

Among the ravage I saw unbelievable courage and beauty from people I suddenly felt an even stronger connection to. One of them was Jolie. At the end of a long day, through the lens of my camera, I captured her pulling a red dress out of the wreckage of her bedroom. Her eyes lit up. She brushed the dress off, slipped out of her torn T-shirt and sweats and slipped on the dress. It flowed down her body in soft, sensuous waves. She rummaged again and managed to dig up a pair of gold heels, which she slipped onto bare feet. We were all going for a simple supper at Jonah's studio, which had remained intact. Our nightly meals had become the highlight of our days. We feasted on rations and spoke of rebuilding. I told Jolie how seeing her in her red dress had touched me.

She smiled. "A long time ago I learned that even in the midst of winter, I am an invincible summer. This dress is my summer, a reminder that things will get better and I will have even more than I did before. This way, I can face anything."

She examined me closely. "What is your summer, Kia? How will you find the courage to face your fears?"

We both glanced at Jonah, seated at the other end of the table.

"I guess my summer has always been my work," I told Jolie.

"Then use your camera to tell him the things you cannot say face-to-face," Jolie suggested.

Taking her advice, I left early. I set up my camera, then curled up in bed and poured my heart out to Jonah. I did love him and it wasn't conditional on him admitting he loved me first. If he didn't, it would hurt but I would survive. Would I leave Haiti if he didn't share my feelings? Was my identity based on him loving me?

I heard the door creak and looked up. Jonah was standing there smiling at me. "I love you, too, Kia."

"How long have you been standing there?" I asked in a breathless voice.

His smile widened. "I followed you home."

I gestured at the camera. "This was just easier for me."

He nodded. "I know how hard it can be. That's why I pretended like it would be okay if you left. The truth is you would've taken a piece of my heart with you."

I held out my arms to him. "I'm not going anywhere."

Before I could catch my breath, I was on my back and Jonah was attacking my breasts, kissing and elongating my nipples before slipping lower. His cascading dreadlocks felt intensely erotic against my skin. He sampled everything in a carnal buffet of human flesh. Slipping his arms under my upper back, he held me tight as he plunged into me. My aching body accepted him greedily. Face-to-face, we stared at each other. His eyes dared me not to look away but to keep myself open, no matter how hard it was to do so.

He grunted with each plunge. I wrapped my legs around his waist, affording him the ability to thrust deeper and harder. He whispered sweet nothings, though his voice was so thick with desire I had trouble understanding his island accent. It made him even more exotic and exciting. I'd never felt so at peace with not being in control of my own body and emotions. I reveled in the brutality of our fuck, in the sheer madness of an intense orgasm ripping through me and the simultaneous outburst from Jonah as we surrendered to a power greater than ourselves.

As Jonah wrapped me up in his arms I realized that, like him, I knew who I was. What I wanted to learn was what I could become with him, what love could do to transform us both. Haiti had become my romance. It was far from a fairy tale, but I was completely spellbound.

RAVEN'S FLIGHT

Andrea Dale

I met Ciaran when he moved in next door to me.

Well, that's not exactly how it happened. One evening there was a camper van parked outside the dilapidated house next door, and then impossibly early the next morning I was rudely awakened by the most god-awful earsplitting noises, and I stormed outside to discover Ciaran on the roof, tearing down the house in preparation for building a new one.

Fortunately for him, he had his shirt off, and the sight choked off the string of expletives I'd drawn in a deep breath to scream.

He had glossy black hair, long enough that he'd drawn it back into a short ponytail; biceps perfect for nibbling on; and then there was the tattoo.

Ink as black as his hair curved and swooped across the muscles of his back. It was Celtic—not the newfangled tribal kind, but the real knot work-from-early-manuscripts kind—and it depicted a raven flying over the ocean, with the sun blazing overhead.

Right then and there, I had the overwhelming compulsion

to lick his tattoo, trace every spiral and intricate knot and line with my tongue.

I wanted it so badly, I trembled, deep inside.

Then, as if sensing someone was watching (where "watching" translates to "lusting nearly to the point of leaping over the fence and tackling"), he turned.

He was as beautiful from the front as he was from the back.

"Well, then," he said, "what have we here?"

I caught how his "th" sounded like "t" and nearly swooned. All that *and* an Irish lilt? Lord and lady, help me.

He gazed down at me appraisingly, one eyebrow raised, and I realized something else.

I'd stormed out of the house wearing nothing but what I wear to bed, which is to say, next to nothing: a soft, faded purple T-shirt that barely brushed the tops of my thighs, and panties that might not be actually visible thanks to the angle of his view.

It was not the best outfit for chewing someone out for waking me up at six a.m., no matter how delicious he was and how tingly he made me. I scowled, turned and stomped back into the house to find more appropriate attire.

To make matters worse, Ciaran—who wiped his hand on his jeans and shook mine politely when he introduced himself—was apologetic and solicitous.

"It's the bloody jet lag," he said. "I'm still wakin' up at four o'clock in ta morning. It didn't even occur to me that someone would be sleeping."

I explained that I was the evening editor at the local paper, so I had weird hours. I didn't explain what I wanted to do with his tattoo—and him. Yet.

Please. I waited almost a week for that. It wasn't easy, but I was strong.

In the meantime, on my day off I offered him a beer as the sun set, and I stood in his ruined yard while he paced around and described how the new house would look. It would be built of redwood and stone and have a tower. The deck would overlook the sunset. There'd be a Jacuzzi on it.

He was an architect and had designed the place himself, with modifications for various planning committees. He'd be doing some of the building himself, too, and he apologized in advance for the noise and mess. I told him as long as the noise didn't start before ten a.m., I could live with it, because his house would probably raise the neighborhood's property values.

He laughed at that, and the skin at the edges of his eyes crinkled, and I nearly jumped him right there. But I restrained myself and tried not to think about him restraining me, which was fantasy number two, right after the tattoo tongue tracing.

The next morning he showed up at my house at a respectable eleven o'clock with coffee and Krispy Kremes. I thought that was right neighborly of him. I was really starting to like this guy. My only minor disappointment was that he was wearing a shirt.

A few nights later I came home after work and saw him sitting on top of his camper van in the light of the full moon, holding up a chalice, and it was all over for me. I climbed up there and celebrated with him, and bathed in the moonlight, we finally kissed.

Those silver-tongued Irish know how to kiss, oh, yes indeedy.

His tongue was soft and slow, exploring my mouth, tasting me. He tasted peaty and smoky like the whiskey from his chalice, which he'd shared with me. He cradled one hand behind my head as he increased the pressure. I felt the sweep of his tongue in a full-body shiver. My nipples peaked, my clit trembled. All that, just from a kiss.

A kiss that rocked my world so soundly, I half thought we were having an earthquake.

So I did what any right-minded hussy would: I took him home with me, and I confessed my burning need to explore his tattoo.

He raised his head from his thorough examination of my collarbone and its environs and laughed softly.

"Oh, is that what you'd be wanting?" he said, his dark eyes flashing. "Never let it be said that Ciaran Moss would deny a lady her greatest wish." In one smooth move he pulled his T-shirt over his head, then stood and shucked out of his soft, worn jeans and underwear. When he stretched himself out on the bed, I saw why he'd stripped completely: the lowest waves lapped at the curve where his lower back met his firm, oh-so-fine buttcheeks.

I divested myself of my own clothes, so we wouldn't have to worry about it later. I may be a hussy, but I'm a practical one. I swept my hair back into a ponytail to keep it out of my way.

Then I straddled his upper thighs, leaned forward and planted my hands on either side of his shoulders on the bed.

Close up, the tattoo was even more fabulous. The lines were true and sure, and the artist had added shading to give the knot work almost a 3-D effect.

I started at the top, with the sun on his right shoulder blade. The rays reached to the base of his neck, tickled his spine. I tasted each one. Ciaran had showered after working on the demolition today, obviously, but beneath the hint of clean soap, there was a hint of salty flesh.

He propped his head on his arms, facing sideways, and I could see his contented smile. As I traced the lines, speeding up a little in the swoops and swirls, he sighed, shifting beneath me a little.

As for me, I was getting wet in all the right places. As I stretched to reach the uppermost lines, my pointed nipples grazed along his back, and we both liked that. Still, I took my time, wanting to savor every inch of that glorious, magical picture.

When I finally got down to the lowest lines, the ocean waves, I gripped his butt for support—and, of course, for my own pleasure and his. He had a runner's ass, lean and hard like the rest of him, with side dimples you could drink champagne from.

Hmm. I made a mental note to try that sometime.

I kneaded gently as I tasted those final lines, and as I finished, we both sighed. I couldn't resist a playful nip on one asscheek, and he flexed and jumped, then somehow flipped over beneath me, leaving me wondering just who was in charge here, even as I remained on top of him.

His cock was a glorious thing, long and lean and hard like the rest of him. I didn't get much time to examine it, actually, because he dipped his fingers down and discovered how wet I was, and we both decided that any more foreplay was both unnecessary and redundant.

Hands on my hips, he guided me over his cock, as if I needed help. In a way, I did—I was shivering with need and half-blind with desire.

"Oh, yes," he said, half a groan and half a whisper, "there's a girl."

"Oh, yes," I echoed, sinking down on the length of him.

The intricate lines of his tattoo danced in my memory as I moved up and down on him, rocked back and forth. At the same time, when I could keep my eyes from fluttering shut, I was drinking in the sight of the sharp planes of his cheekbones, the spread of his black hair on my pale green sheets, the way his eyes darkened to blue-black.

With his hands he urged me to rock back and forth, then reached to toy with my nipples, teasing me harder as he watched my reaction. When he pinched them, the sudden near-pain sent me over the edge, cresting like the ocean waves along his waist.

He flipped me over so he could take control, and I most obligingly wrapped my legs around his waist. He leaned forward so he could kiss me again, nipping my lower lip, his soft hair brushing my skin. He said something I couldn't understand—Gaelic, I supposed—but it sounded like a blessing.

Then he started to move inside me, and all I could say was his name, over and over, until finally I couldn't form words at all. His hands closed gently around my wrists, holding them down against the bed, and it was enough to send me flying again.

This time, he took wing and joined me.

He told me in detail about his tattoo, what each part of it meant to him. His totem was the raven, the waves represented his journey, and the sun meant he would always be able to find home. We shared the same spiritual beliefs, and it all made perfect sense to me.

I asked, a little worried, if my fetish about licking his tattoo was disrespectful, and he told me that love was the greatest act of worship.

I'll drink to that.

It was a year later—his new house almost finished, but he'd been living in mine for most of that time and really, we were calling it ours—when I said, "I want to get a tattoo."

I'd toyed with the idea before, and I knew I'd know when the time was right. I knew what I wanted, but I wouldn't tell him. I wanted him to be with me when I got it done, though. That was a given.

The pain wasn't as bad as I expected—getting my legs waxed

hurt a hell of a lot more, although that was usually over faster. I stared in fascination as the needle emblazoned my skin with the feeling of a razor blade lightly tracing my flesh, at the little beads of blood that rose to the surface, only to be wiped away. Then I closed my eyes and meditated on how my life had changed, on how the cycles turned and came around again.

Ciaran held my other hand, quietly, respectfully. When I squeezed his fingers, he gently squeezed back, and when I opened my eyes, he was smiling at me, a look akin to wonder on his face.

The tattoo was of my own design, of course—Ciaran and I agreed that nothing was more ridiculous than choosing #5 off the wall. On the underside of my left wrist was a full moon with a spiral in the center. Around my wrist, connecting with the moon, twined a band of ivy.

Two weeks later, the house was finished and my tattoo was healed. We sat on the deck watching the setting sun, and Ciaran took my hand in his and slowly began tracing the spiral with his tongue. The underside of the wrist is a pretty sensitive place already, you know? I swear my eyes rolled into the back of my head.

But he wouldn't let me go and pushed my other hand away when I reached for the buttons of his jeans. No, he made me wait, shaking with desire, as he languorously dampened every millimeter of my tattoo. This is how he must have felt, I realized hazily, the first time—maybe every time—I licked his tattoo: desperate with want, aching with need.

He carried me upstairs to the heavy wrought iron bed and told me to imagine that my tattoo bound my wrist to the head-board. I grabbed the cold iron with both hands, and he loosely wrapped a tie around the other wrist. Bound by imagination and craving, I let him explore my body the way he had the tattoo, with hands and mouth, until I pled with him for release.

When he gave it to me, I wasn't clutching the bed anymore, but Ciaran himself, soaring with him once again.

There are two ravens on Ciaran's back now, flying together over the waves and beneath the sun.

Tonight I'm going to tell him he should start thinking about maybe adding a little leaping salmon in the waves. I'd better have a shot of whiskey ready for him....

RAINDROPS
AND ROOFTOPS

Elizabeth Coldwell

It was just another Friday in the office, until Marilyn wandered over to tell me I was going to New York. I checked the desk calendar to make sure it wasn't April 1st, then waited for her to explain.

When I'd first joined *Fresh Destinations* as junior features writer, my friends had been deeply envious. They'd assumed—as I had—that the fact I was working on a travel magazine meant I'd be regularly jetting off to exotic locations to write about the best new hotels and spa resorts. What I hadn't realized was that the senior staff members had first pick of the plum assignments. In the five months I'd been working here, the farthest I'd traveled on behalf of the magazine was Luxembourg, which is every bit as exciting as it sounds. The trip to cover the opening of New York's latest boutique hotel had been earmarked for Jilly, the features editor, who had only recently returned from a two-week safari in Kenya.

"I got a call from Jilly's husband a few minutes ago," Marilyn was saying. "She's been diagnosed with malaria, would you believe? That's why you should always take all your medication before you travel."

I bit back the urge to ask exactly what tropical disease I might have contracted on my weekend in Luxembourg. I was too busy thinking about all the extra work that would be piled on me in Jilly's absence.

"It's thrown all my plans into disarray, I can tell you, Keeley. Who'd be an editor, eh? Most importantly, it means I need someone to be on that flight to JFK this evening. So...pack your bags, you're going to the Big Apple."

I almost hugged her. "Thank you so much. You can rely on me to do this properly. I won't let you down, I promise." Mentally compiling a list of everything I needed to take, I was halfway to the door before I realized I'd left my jacket hanging over the back of my chair. Marilyn smiled at me as I scuttled back to collect it, but I knew she was already wondering whether she'd made the correct decision.

When I collected the ticket that was waiting for me at the airline information desk, I had my second shock of the day. I hadn't realized I was going to be traveling business class, but I gave the woman behind the desk a nonchalant smile, as though this was an everyday occurrence for me.

The feeling of unreality persisted long after I'd taken my seat in the half-empty business section. I wasn't used to the polite attentiveness of the flight attendants, the constant offers of another drink, the beautifully prepared in-flight meal. I was fighting the urge to tell someone this was all a mistake and I should really be sitting in the sardine-can confines of economy class. There was a name for what I was experiencing; I'd seen it in some magazine article. They called it "imposter syndrome":

the belief that you were in a situation, even an entire career, under false pretenses, and at any moment you would be found out and returned to your proper station in life.

A handsome blond flight attendant walked past my seat. "Everything okay there, miss?" he asked in a voice that held more than a trace of the Deep South. As I gazed into his azure eyes I had the urge to confess—though not to the feeling that, deep down, I had no right to be here. Instead, I wanted to tell him he was inspiring some very naughty thoughts in me. Thoughts in which I took hold of his dark uniform tie and led him to the toilets, where I would let him ease down my panties and lick me to a beautiful orgasm, secure in the knowledge this was business class and there wouldn't be an irate queue of passengers waiting outside for us to finish. From the way he was looking at me, I reckoned his thoughts might be running along very similar lines.

A woman toward the front of the cabin pressed her call button. He turned to see what she wanted and the spell was broken. But as he moved smoothly down the aisle, I realized our brief eye contact had shown me something very important. This weekend, I could be anyone I wanted to be: the kind of girl who had a wild encounter with a cute flight attendant in midair or spent the night with a horny stranger, knowing she would never see him again. All the things I would never dream of doing in my everyday life. Head whirling with so many delicious possibilities, I settled back to enjoy the rest of the flight.

The Dunbar Hotel was in the heart of Manhattan's theater district, a couple of blocks from Times Square. Gazing out of the limo window at the rush-hour traffic on Broadway, I felt a surge of excitement in my stomach. The scene was so familiar from countless movies and TV shows, with a never-ending stream of Yellow Cabs on the road and women in business suits and trainers bustling past on the pavement—or sidewalk, as I supposed I had to think of it now.

At last, the car pulled up outside the hotel, and the uniformed chauffeur opened the door for me. The PR firm behind the Dunbar's launch was clearly pulling out all the stops to make sure the invited members of the press had a memorable weekend. Check-in was swift, and my bags were taken up to my room on the third floor by a chatty bellboy. The press release for the hotel described it as "an oasis of urban cool." In the case of the room I was now looking at, that seemed to translate into ergonomically designed furniture, gunmetal gray bedcovers and a tiny en suite wet room. There was a bowl of complimentary popcorn on the desk. I munched on a handful as I unpacked. The itinerary I'd been given told me there was a drinks reception in what had been wittily titled the Dun-bar in less than thirty minutes, which just about gave me time to shower and change into the cocktail dress I'd brought with me.

As I applied a slick of lip gloss, I looked my reflection squarely in the eye and said, "You belong here, and you deserve any adventures that come your way." Then I reached up under my skirt, removed my panties and tossed them on the bed. Even if no one else discovered my secret, it gave me a thrill to know that I was wearing no underwear.

Almost all the other guests were already in the bar when I entered. Waiters stood holding champagne flutes on silver trays. I helped myself to one and took a sip to steady my nerves. The bar itself had been designed to run the full length of the room, bottles arranged artfully against the mirrored back wall. The leather couches were low slung and comfortable looking, and salsa music playing from hidden speakers reinforced the impression this was somewhere to come if you wanted to see and be seen.

I looked around for a friendly face to talk to. I couldn't spot the hotel's PR woman, and it seemed most of the journalists here already knew each other from previous press trips. They were engaged in conversations about people and events I couldn't hope to make any sense of. Suddenly, I felt very out of place, imposter syndrome kicking in with a vengeance once more.

Floor-to-ceiling windows gave a stunning view out on to the street below. I walked over to them and stood gazing out into the night. Raindrops chased each other down the glass, blurring and softening the colors of the neon signs on the buildings across the way.

"So, your first time in New York, eh?" an American-accented voice behind me asked. I turned to discover one of the most gorgeous men I'd ever seen smiling at me. Somewhere in his late thirties, he had dark hair thickly streaked with gray, intelligent hazel eyes and an intriguing little scar just above his top lip. As he reached for a glass of champagne, I noticed a watch that probably cost more than I earned in a year adorning his wrist. That and his stylishly tailored suit suggested someone at the top of his profession—probably a writer for one of the Sunday broadsheets.

"Is it really that obvious?" I replied.

"Well, you're standing on your own, admiring the view. Everyone else is more concerned about getting their glass refilled." He took a sip from his own drink before continuing, "And what do you think of the hotel?"

"I'm not sure," I replied. "In some respects, the design feels like it's trying a bit too hard, but I do love this bar. It's the sort of place I'd want to come if I was meeting friends for a night on the town." On impulse, I stuck out a hand for him to shake. "Keeley Carter, *Fresh Destinations*."

He took my hand, his touch sending a rush of lust straight to my core. "Adam Dunbar."

I knew then I'd committed a terrible *faux pas*. I'd expressed a less than complimentary opinion of the hotel to the man who owned it. If Marilyn learned about this, she would never send me on another press trip. "I'm sorry," I said. "What I said about the hotel..."

"Don't worry about it. I like your honesty." He glanced around at the assembled journalists. The volume of their chatter was rising audibly as their glasses were refilled. "I get the feeling everyone else I talk to tonight is just going to tell me what they think I want to hear."

He was still holding my hand, only now his thumb was gently stroking the soft skin on the inside of my wrist; such an intimate caress, from someone who barely knew me. Did that mean he'd felt the same spark as I had when he first touched me?

Adam smiled wickedly. "If you think the view from here is good, you really need to see it from higher up. Come on, let me show you."

"Aren't you supposed to be mingling with your guests?" I asked.

"Supposed to be, but I don't really think they'll miss me."

How could I refuse? How could I tell myself I deserved an adventure, then turn one down when it was offered to me? I let Adam lead me out of the room, expecting him to head for the elevators. Instead, he took me down the corridor and pushed open a door that let out onto a flight of stairs. "It's going to be a bit of a climb," he warned me, "but it's the best way to reach the roof."

He had to be joking, I thought, but as we began the ascent I soon realized he was utterly serious. By the time we'd climbed a good half-dozen floors my thighs ached and I was beginning to wonder what I'd let myself in for. But when Adam pushed down on the bar that released the fire door at the top of the stairs, I realized it had all been worth it.

I stepped out onto the roof of the building, my breath catching in my throat as I saw the majesty of the cityscape around me. Looking downtown, I could see the distinctive peaks of the Chrysler Building and the Empire State Building, along with a forest of skyscrapers I couldn't put a name to, vast glass and steel columns pushing up defiantly toward the heavens. Below us, the traffic noise was a constant hum, punctuated by the sudden whoop of a fire siren.

"This is incredible," I breathed, hardly noticing the steadily falling rain. Adam was watching me, an amused expression on his face. "Thank you for showing me this."

"No, thank *you* for being willing to climb all those stairs in your heels without complaining. You can't know how refreshing that is, compared to most of the women I know...."

He took me in his arms and kissed me, a soft, affectionate kiss that slowly deepened into something more passionate. Things were moving faster than I was used to, but Adam seemed to sense, as I did, that we didn't have much time. I was a visitor in his country, a guest in his hotel, and in less than thirty-six hours I would be leaving again. Whirlwind didn't begin to describe this romance.

And it was romantic, crazily so, to be standing on a New York rooftop in the rain, sharing kisses with a man I'd only just met. My hands roved down his body, feeling the muscles beneath the designer clothing. His mouth worked its way along my neck and into the hollow of my throat as I sagged against him, weak with the depth of my desire for him.

Eventually, he gazed deep into my eyes. "I could do this all night, but you're getting wet..."

The double meaning in his words was obvious to both of us. Water was dripping from the ends of my hair and my dress was almost soaked through, but I hardly noticed. I was consumed by the liquid heat between my legs, and the need to be touched there. As my body pressed against Adam's, I'd felt his hard cock, trapped beneath his clothing and ready to be freed. My fingers itched to unzip him and bring that cock out to play, but Adam had other ideas.

"I haven't put anyone in the honeymoon suite," he said. He must have seen my startled expression because he said, "Yes, I know that doesn't seem to fit in with my vision for the hotel, but this isn't just any honeymoon suite, Keeley, I promise you."

We slipped back through the fire door, Adam pulling it securely shut behind him. One flight of stairs down, Adam led me into the corridor. He produced a card key from his pocket and used it to open the first room we came to. Whatever I'd been expecting, it wasn't the sumptuous drapes and bed that looked big enough to accommodate three people, never mind a loved-up pair of newlyweds. The lighting was soft, subdued, more akin to candlelight, and the air in the room was perfumed with the sensuous scent of jasmine. It was the kind of room you never wanted to leave, where you could shut the door behind you and forget anyone else existed but the two of you.

While I stood gawping, Adam had been into the bathroom, returning with a fluffy white bath sheet that I used to towel dry my hair.

"More champagne?" he asked, opening a concealed door in the wall by the bed to reveal a small fridge containing two half-bottles of vintage bubbly. "When the couple book the room, we'll always ask them how they'd like this fridge to be stocked. Champagne, Armagnac, vintage wine...and we'll also give them the choice of the nice hamper or the naughty one."

Now I was intrigued. I took the glass Adam handed to me, kicked off my shoes and spread the towel on the bedcover before sitting down on it. "And what do they get when they choose?"

Adam launched into his speech with relish. "The nice hamper is, shall we say, the more vanilla choice. Everything the true romantic could crave. Handmade chocolates, strawberries, massage oil, an ostrich feather duster for those who like a little tickle and tease...."

Vanilla it might have been, but the images Adam was planting in my mind were causing me to squirm against the towel, rubbing my thighs together to create the friction my pussy was craving. I pictured him stripped naked and leaning over me as I lay on the bed, running the feathers over the crests of my nipples and down the length of my body to brush tormentingly lightly over my mound before beginning their upward progress once more. He'd repeat the process till I was a flushed, helpless mess, begging for him to touch me where I was almost desperate for it.

With an effort, I brought myself back to the moment, aware that Adam was watching me with wry amusement. "What about the naughty box?"

"Oh, that's for people who want something more spicy, more adventurous with their romance. I believe I have one here, if you'd like to see it."

Adam brought a lacquered box out from another cupboard, producing from its depths a foil-wrapped candy. He unwrapped it and put it to my lips. It was good-quality dark chocolate; when I bit into the liquid center, I tasted the heat of chili.

Adam pressed his lips hard to mine, kissing the burn away. "Not what you were expecting, huh?" His smile was wolfish. "And all the more exciting for it, I'll bet."

"Mm..." I was eager to know what other delights the box contained.

"Help yourself," Adam offered, following the line of my gaze.

I fished out more chocolates, flavored condoms, a bottle of strawberry-scented lube, handcuffs lined with fake fur and something I didn't recognize—a thin wand of soft silicone rubber with half-a-dozen balls molded into its length. I flexed it curiously.

"Some people call them love pearls," Adam said. "They're anal beads. You insert them in your lover's ass and pull them out at the moment of climax. Blows their mind..."

I tried to work out if he was speaking from experience. At the same time, I couldn't help but wonder how it might feel to have that bizarre-looking toy in my own ass. I'd never tried anal play, probably because no man had ever been able to convince me it might be a good idea. Until now.

"I don't make a habit of fucking women I've only just met," Adam told me, "but I know that if I don't do this now, you'll be gone from my life before I have the chance to ask you again. Keeley, I can't let this moment slip away...."

"Neither can I." Now I knew why I didn't feel like I belonged downstairs with the rest of the press pack. It was because my place was here, if only for tonight, with this luscious man. The obvious uncertainty beneath his sophisticated exterior, his fear of coming on too strong and scaring me away, only made me want him more.

Our mouths met once again, and Adam's hand worked its way in slow, teasing circles up beneath my skirt. I found my breath growing shorter as he moved nearer to my pussy. When he registered my lack of panties, his eyes widened. "I knew I was right to open the naughty box," he murmured.

His other hand reached for the zipper of my dress, pulling it down. I wriggled out of the dress as he removed his own clothes. When he was down to a pair of black boxer shorts, he spread my legs wide and settled himself between them. The first touch of his mouth on my pussy had me arching my back with pleasure. Adam clearly loved to lick a woman there; his tongue strokes were flat and sweeping one moment, delicate and precise the next. Each long sweep was getting me wet all the way down to the pucker of my ass, and I knew this was the first stage in preparing me for what he'd called the love pearls.

Soon, I was clutching handfuls of the bedcovers and pushing my hips up toward his mouth, certain that only a little more pressure on my clit would have me coming. That was when Adam knelt up and reached for the lube.

"Not just yet, sweetheart," he said, sensing my frustration. "The wait will be worth it, I promise you."

He urged me up on to hands and knees, then I felt lube being squeezed over my ass, sliding gently down my cleft like an intimate caress. When Adam's finger rubbed gently at my asshole, I sighed, giving him every encouragement to go farther. He pressed a little harder. For a moment I thought I wouldn't yield, then I felt him slip inside. My response was somewhere between a gasp and a giggle.

"Good girl." Adam lavished kisses on the nape of my neck and my shoulders. All the while, his finger was working a little deeper, opening me a little more. When he judged I was ready, he withdrew his fingers, then that wicked wand was pushing in to take its place.

"Ohhh..." The initial discomfort was fading, replaced by pure pleasure. I'd never felt anything like it. Those lumps and bumps were stimulating me in sensitive spots I didn't even know I had. If this was naughtiness, I wanted more of it.

Adam broke off, and I heard the sound of a condom wrapper

being torn. When I looked over my shoulder, I saw him sheathing himself in thin green latex. *Mint flavor,* I thought.

Not that I got the chance to taste it. He got behind me again, clutching me by the hips and guiding himself into my cunt. His cock wasn't the thickest I'd known, but combined with those wicked silicone beads it made me feel fuller than I'd ever been. When he started to thrust, slow and steady, I knew neither of us would last long. He was being stimulated by the sight of the toy sticking out of my ass and the feel of its contours every time he pushed in and slid out. I was playing with my own clit, experiencing the little sparks of sensation in my belly that let me know my orgasm wasn't very far away.

"That's good...so good," I babbled, as Adam moved the pace at which he was fucking me smoothly up the gears. Something seemed to catch and release deep inside me, and I yelled that I was coming.

That was the signal for Adam to pull the beads from my ass. The way they felt going in was nothing compared to the moment they popped out of me. It was like I was coming unglued. I barely registered Adam's climax, triggered by my cunt and ass clenching in rhythm.

I couldn't frame the words to thank Adam for what had been the most incredible sex of my life. He lay beside me, stroking the hair from my eyes and occasionally kissing me softly.

"That was too good to only be a one-time thing," he declared, pulling me into an embrace under the covers.

I was thinking exactly the same thing. This was simply going to be my little adventure, my chance to prove I belonged in this world of press junkets and five-star luxury. If only Adam hadn't turned out to be the kind of man I could so very easily fall in love with. "But perhaps that's all it was meant to be," I said. "After all, I have to go back to London very soon."

"And I have to go there, too. I'm very keen to expand my chain, and where better to open a new Dunbar hotel than London?" He smiled. "I get the feeling I'm going to spend rather more time researching the ideal location than I thought. It's very important I get it right...."

I could barely keep from grinning like an idiot as Adam outlined his plans, all of which seemed to include me.

"Meanwhile," he finished, "we have the rest of the night together. I mean, it would be a shame not to sample the whole honeymoon suite experience. The breakfast in bed is very good here, and the staff is extremely discreet...."

Reaching down between his legs, I discovered he was already getting hard again. I couldn't resist one last glimpse into the night, from the windows where we had neglected to close the drapes. The rain was still falling on this amazing city, and I couldn't wait to see where my adventure with Adam would take me next.

TOPIARY

K. D. Grace

I sn't it time yet? Surely it must be."

Aden ignores me, lost in concentration, delicately clip-clipping the unruly new growth from a perfectly spiraling boxwood.

I can always find him beyond the hedged labyrinth surrounded by fantastical shapes and patterns all sculpted in evergreen, each time a new shrub, each time a new shape. Aden is an artist when it comes to shrubs. He hired me to do the kitchen garden. I grow vegetables. I don't understand his fascination. But there's no denying Aden is the Topiary King.

"Surely it must be time." I squirm on the stone bench, feeling the discomfort of my condition.

"These things can't be rushed, Bess. All gardeners know that." He's working gloveless, like always. He says he needs to feel what he does. No one would ever believe what delicate work he can do with hands so hard. With his thumb and first two fingers he patiently teases and coaxes out the tiniest of wayward shoots until the hard swell of a budding leaf close to the top of the spiraling shrub is visible, something no one else would have noticed.

As I watch him, I bear down against the cool stone of the bench and shift from buttock to buttock. The nip of the secateurs is crisp, precise, and I catch my breath with a little moan. "At least check. Please."

His shoulders rise and fall in a sigh of resignation. His eyes still on the shrub, checking for other unruly bits to be tamed, he carefully lays down the secateurs and slowly, still studying his efforts, moves toward me.

I brace against the bench and shift my weight backward, ready for him.

"Timing is everything," he lectures. "There has to be enough growth to do what I envision, and what I envision must be there already waiting to be exposed."

I lean back a little, feeling the clench and the flutter in my pussy that comes from knowing it's almost time. I can barely stand another second of the heaviness, the chaos. I long for order, his order, which he never gives until conditions are just right. Please, dear god, let conditions be just right. My impatience feels heavy and swollen like the buds Aden examines and caresses and nips.

"Open up."

I do as I'm told. He kneels in front of me and pushes chlorophyll-stained fingers under my skirt. He's hard. He's always hard when he shapes the shrubs. The first time he fucked me, he'd been shaping the same spiraling boxwood. He burst into the kitchen garden while I was bent over weeding the young carrots. It was all over in a few minutes, me gasping my orgasm with my shorts around my ankles, and him hammering into me, coming in hard shudders. Now, most of the time he lingers, like he does with his shrubs. The memory makes me clench and rock against the bench.

I feel heat rising off him. I smell his sweat all piquant and woodsy. I'm so tight and tetchy that even the first graze of his fingertips against my muff makes me gasp and wriggle.

I never had a muff—at least not a real one—until I met Aden. I was smooth and naked. I wore bikinis and thongs. But Aden doesn't like bare ground where something should be growing.

In the beginning it itched. Every night Aden tended me with soothing lotions and oils while he admired my new growth, tiny and prickly like young grass. He promised me it would be worth the wait. With time, the new growth thickened and grew soft and escaped the edges of my panties like it was always migrating toward his touch. The more it grew, the more his hand was there to caress, to examine. Then I stopped trying to contain it. I stopped wearing panties and let Aden's garden grow unhindered. All that soft springy growth was new to me. I could barely keep my hands from straying under my skirt for a stroke. I never missed a chance to admire its rude, rambunctious fullness when I was naked, or when I was in the bathroom. My muff exerted more control over us than I would have ever imagined. One of us was always touching it or talking about it or thinking about it. That led to sex. Lots of sex.

And when we fucked, my god, there was rough, uneven texture that hadn't been there before. It was a primordial act when he fucked me in the topiary. It was fur against fur, catching and holding the animal scent of us, humping and growling and spreading our smell on the grass like the rest of the wildlife.

He shivers his fingers up through my lush growth and sucks his bottom lip in concentration. I practically catapult off the seat as his thumb rakes my clit. "Maybe," he says, shoving in closer until I can feel his breath against my inner thigh. "Could be."

"Please." I squirm against his open palm. "I can't wait much longer."

He shoves at my skirt with an impatient hand, raking and caressing, pushing my legs apart, examining. His nose is scant millimeters away. I know he smells the heat of my pussy. He's close enough to taste me. It takes all of my self-control not to thrust myself full-on at his face.

The frown of concentration hardens to satisfied resolve, and he drops a breathy kiss against my mound. "Wait here, darling. I'll be right back, and don't touch." He slaps my hand away.

It feels like he's gone for ages. I grind my bottom against the stone and imagine penis and pussy shapes in the shrubs of Aden's topiary. When he returns, I practically sob with relief.

"Take off your clothes. All of them." His voice is firm, certain, like he knows exactly what he's about, like he has a plan. He watches as I strip off T-shirt, bra, skirt. My skin goes all goosefleshed with the warm breeze making my body hair stand at attention, making my muff feel bigger than the spiraling boxwood Aden has been tending.

But he doesn't notice the gooseflesh. He doesn't notice the lead weight of my nipples, or my kittenish whimpers. He sees only my verdant dark patch, the patch that now pillows his weight every night when he mounts me, the patch that always makes him hard.

He orders me to straddle the bench and scoot down until I'm sitting at the end, legs splayed wide apart. Then when he's satisfied that I'm right where he wants me, he kneels in front of me and opens a leather case, which contains a comb and several small pairs of scissors. "They're newly sharpened," he says. "I knew you were close. I didn't want to be caught unprepared."

I thrust my hips forward. Everything between my thighs feels expanded and puffy.

At first Aden simply strokes my heavy curls, his face in deep concentration. His creative juices, like my own, are flowing. I begin to thrust lightly against his stroking, impatient for him to get on with it. But he won't be rushed. There's a stroke with the comb here, a shove of my leg there, a shivering with his fingers as he plumps and fluffs. "Yes, I see it now," he breathes. "I know exactly how it's supposed to be."

He begins.

He combs and snips and says half under his breath, "Mm-hm, uh-huh, just a little more. That's right. Perfect." Then he switches to another pair of scissors. I can't tell the difference, but he says he needs to create texture, depth, a sense of perspective.

"The landscape should always showcase its finest feature." His fingers press in around my clit, and he rubs and strokes it to prominence.

I try to sit still as he clips and combs, but I'm slippery and swollen and all of the fantastical shapes in Aden's exquisite topiary now appear orgiastic, spreading wide, thrusting upward, pouting and arching. The bench is damp beneath me and Aden's trousers look as though they're about to lose the battle for containment. He breathes like there's a windstorm in his lungs, and with each snip, he squirms and shifts.

With a weighty grunt, he brushes away the hair he's trimmed and buries his face in my pussy. "Perfect," he says when he comes up for air. Then from inside the case, he pulls a gilt hand mirror just the right size for admiring personal gardens. He holds it up for me to see.

I'm splayed wide on the bench and the dark red of my pout swells like a wet cavern beneath the delicate bonsai sculpting of my curls. As I admire his artistic skills, Aden frees his cock from his trousers and the naked weight of it presses insistently against my thigh.

"Very nice." His breath steams the mirror, obliterating the view of my private topiary. Then he pulls me off the bench onto his lap, wriggling and positioning until his cock is pressing between my labia. He holds me there just long enough to torture us both. Then he thrusts into me, all the way in, and I'm slick and gripping as he rolls me onto the grass.

He rakes across my pubic landscape with each thrust, and he does it slowly so we can both feel the texture and the depth of what he's created in my bush. "Perfect, exquisite," he grunts. "Can you feel it? Can you feel how it changes everything?" He arches upward and runs his hand down between us to fondle his work. "The angle is now better for penetration. It makes no sense, I know, but it is. Can you feel it? And your clit is now better exposed for stimulation." He tweaks my clit and I nearly buck him off for his efforts. He chuckles at my sensitivity, then rubs against me. I lift my legs and wrap them around him, and we come together.

There's a view of the topiary from the patio. We eat there in the evening. We eat salmon and new potatoes, then feed each other strawberries fresh from the kitchen garden. Beneath the table, Aden wriggles his bare foot up under my skirt. I slump in my chair and go all vacant-eyed while I bear down against the press of him until I come in gasps and shudders as his toes circle my clit and dip into my pout. Then he beckons me to him and pulls me onto his lap like he's Santa Claus and I'm trying to convince him I've been a good little girl. But Santa Claus has a raging hard-on, and I'm definitely not a good little girl.

I wake from my sex-crazed dream. Sunlight streams through the bedroom window, there's water running in the bathroom. I yawn and stretch and shove myself into a sitting position against muscles that are tender from the celebration of my pubic sculpting. It began on the patio, then moved into the topiary under the full moon. At some point, we ended up sweating and grunting in the middle of Aden's big bed.

"Darling? Are you up?" Aden calls. "I've drawn your bath."

I don't bother with a robe. I shuffle into the bathroom displaying Aden's masterpiece proudly between my legs. He's waiting next to the tub full of lavender-scented water, lavender that I've no doubt grown for him. I'm surprised to find him dressed in his gardening clothes. He barely notices his artwork as he takes my hand and helps me into the tub. I'm a bit confused, but it's early and my brain is still pretty sex addled. I lie back and close my eyes. He sponges me all over, lingering to lick the water droplets off my breasts. Then while he slides the sponge between my legs, washing the parts of me that are still tender and raw from last night's orgy, he fellates my toes one by one, and when he's finished, I'm spread wide and ready, grinding my bottom against the marble tub, not caring how bruised my pussy is. I want him.

But when I reach for his fly, he pushes my hands away. "Not yet, Bess. There's something I have to do first."

I offer him a pouty little whimper, which he ignores as he takes my hand and helps me to stand. Then he begins to wash my sculpted pubes, soaping them until they're white, pressed to jagged sudsy peaks like small glaciers. Running his fingers through my sudsed curls seems endlessly fascinating to him, so I stand in growing impatience with my legs open and my pussy gaping to be filled.

And still he lathers me.

"Aden, please," I beg. "I need you to fuck me."

"Not just yet." His voice sounds like it does when he's in the topiary, concentrating hard on his latest creation.

"Aden?"

It's then I notice the razor on the countertop and I nearly lose my balance in a tidal wave of water that drenches both of us. But Aden steadies me. "Stand still, darling." He reaches for the razor. "One day's growth can change everything. With one day's growth I can see how I might have done better, how I could do better next time."

"Next time? But—"

"Sh-sh-sh." He feasts on my mouth until I'm unable to protest, until he knows I'll do whatever he wants. Then his words come in a breathless rush. "Listen to me, darling, yesterday was just our first attempt. It was a magnificent attempt, granted, but think of what we can create once we've had a little practice." He's hard, nearly to bursting, as he lays two fingers against my labia. I hold my breath as he gently makes the first scrape with the razor. "It'll only be bare for a little while," he reassures me.

I watch through a mist of tears as in a matter of minutes he scrapes away his lovely creation, which has taken me months to grow. At last I'm smooth and naked once more. "A blank slate," he whispers, as he rinses away the last of the soap and bends to kiss the naked skin.

I stand crying quietly while he towels me dry. All the while he speaks softly to me, comforting me, promising me that next time it will be even better.

He carries me back to the bed and soothes my rawness with luxurious lotion, massaging in slow, even strokes that end with his thumb circling my clit. I quiver against him and lift my bottom to show him what I need.

"You'll see, love," he breathes. "It'll grow back so quickly and so beautifully." He stands to undress. "When it does, it'll be good. So good."

When he pushes into me, I feel the hungry rub of him against my new nakedness, and even through my loss, I find myself already anticipating the itch of new growth.

I WANT TO
HOLD YOUR
HAND

Rachel Kramer Bussel

Shelly looked over at her husband, Ron, across their gleaming lawn, finding him instantly amidst their party guests. She smiled slightly, then set her lips into a straight line; not a frown, but more of an adjustment. Adjustments were what she'd been making for the last two years, ever since he set out to, and did, lose over a hundred pounds, going from severely overweight to big but in shape, the kind of guy who could help push a car out of the snow or carry a heavy box or other tasks that required bulk, strength, power. Now instead of being fat and cuddly, a sexy teddy bear of a giant, he was more like a line-backer, thick and stocky—and sexy, at least, by conventional standards. While it seemed to Shelly that men had more leeway than women in acceptable weight gain, the old Ron had crossed over into invisibility in the sex appeal department, though not for her—never for her. Now, people, especially women, were fawning over him like he'd cured cancer, while she, in her same old not-too-big, not-too-small size-six jeans, smiled along, trying to adjust to the new man she was now married to.

The truth was, she had preferred him bigger; it went with his outsized personality, not to mention the way he held her down in bed, the way he kept her warm, the way she curved up against him, the way he looked at her, like he was the Tarzan to her Jane. Now, even though technically he weighed more than her, Shelly had trouble getting into that same submissive mindset, perhaps because his personality seemed to have changed too. She didn't like to think that all the recent adoration had gone to his head, but maybe it had, because even when he was on top of her, even when he pressed her hips deep into the mattress the way she liked it, even when he spooned her at night, curling up around her, she couldn't quite recapture the magic. She wanted to, but she liked her men bigger, brawnier, huskier. It was hard to fantasize about him being the brute who ravaged her when she could sense that soon she'd be able to feel his ribs. Soon she might not be able to pinch the inches she so welcomed, and would have to twist and squirm to find ways to fit into him, rather than just next to him. She still loved Ron and had no intention of leaving him, but seeing all the girls fawning over his new muscles made her want to gag. Where had they been when he'd stared unhappily at himself naked in the mirror, when there was nothing she could do to make him see what she saw in him? She felt like the heart of their relationship had slipped away along with the pounds; why didn't Weight Watchers ever tell you about this possible side effect?

At least he had two body parts that hadn't lost their heft: his hands and his cock. She knew that saying about a man's feet predicting his size below the waist, but with Ron, his hands and his cock were both, well, manly, while his size-nine feet were what she considered average. His hands, though, were big, strong, powerful; there was nothing he could do about his man hands. Ron had always been able to speak to her with his hands, even on their first date, when he'd reached for one of hers and massaged it, his thumb tricking along her palm, his fingers tickling her skin, making her curious about him, about what he could do to her. They were soft, and seemingly tender, but when she dared to try to get to know them, he'd crushed her fingers within his own, letting her know that he would be the one to master their manual dexterity.

She was still curious, as she'd been then, eager to get to know him by running her lips along his skin, by listening to his heartbeat, though the parts that everyone else was so eager to talk about and salivate over were not the ones that interested Shelly. His abs, his biceps, all sounded like clichés to her ears. Her Ron wasn't the macho bodybuilder they were making him out to be, and if he were, she wasn't sure she would want him anymore. She'd caught a couple of college girls, home on break, whispering about what he might look like underneath his clothes, and had huffed her way through their conversation, stalking right in between them and giving them the stink eye. Who were these brats and why didn't they find someone their own age?

"Honey, I want to go to the movies," she said, pulling him aside, not caring how petulant she might sound.

"Now?" He looked at her in confusion.

"Well, tonight, yeah."

"What do you want to see?"

"I don't care," she said, then lifted his right hand and brought it to her mouth. With that, she sucked on his index finger, making sure his eyes stayed on hers, taking it all the way before releasing it to lick his palm, not caring if any of their guests saw. Let them watch; let them see that she wasn't impressed by Ron's trimmer body, but by the things she knew his body could do, things that had nothing to do with how much he weighed. She knew what she was doing tickled from the way his hand quivered, and she liked making him squirm. Then she moved down to his wrist, where she thought she could feel his pulse racing. "I just want to hold your hand. You know, like we used to."

It sounded innocent enough, but they'd done a lot more than hand holding back in the day. There was one movie date in particular she recalled, though not the actual movie itself. They'd gone to the theater at 12th and 2nd Avenue in the East Village, during the middle of the afternoon, back when they'd lived in the city, rather than the 'burbs in Jersey. It hadn't been too crowded, with just a smattering of people. She'd been sitting on the aisle and he'd been next to her, his arm taking over the armrest—not that she minded. Shelley was drawn to Ron for his size, for what it symbolized, for how he used it. He could dominate her space any time, especially when his hand reached for hers and then held it, lightly at first, but enough to let the pressure seep into other parts of her body, so it almost seemed as if he were touching her pussy. The tingling increased as he lightly stroked his fingers along her palm, and by the end of the movie, she was shocked she'd been able to restrain herself from dipping her fingers into her panties.

He looked at her and paused, as if she'd said she wanted to go to the movies in Paris. "Baby, what's wrong?"

With those three words, Shelly knew she hadn't lost her man completely to his newfound popularity with the ladies. He could tell, from her innocent-sounding suggestion, what it was she was talking about, and that she wanted an escape. He could tell she didn't mean holding hands like in a romantic 1950s photo, but in a way that signaled so much more. He took her hand in his and squeezed it hard, squeezed all of his love into the press of his palm against hers, his fingers digging deep. He'd lost some of his size, but none of his strength, and when she looked down at their joined hands, she smiled, and reached for his other. They stood there, smiling and squeezing, until he upped the intensity a notch, squeezing so hard her breath came out in gasps.

Trying to ignore the twinges, she sputtered out, "It's just—all these girls—they don't care that you're married, they don't care about who you were before. They just see, well, the new you, and it makes me wonder if we can hold onto *us* when you're so different."

He let go of her hands and she moved into his arms, letting herself relax against his bulk. She smiled as a tear rolled down her cheek, because he was still bulky; she was still shorter and smaller than him and fit into the crook of his arm, even if that arm was more solid and less fleshy than before. Ron patted her smooth hair and let his breath land against her forehead. "I'm not going anywhere, Shell. Those girls...it's flattering, I'm not gonna lie. I've never had that kind of attention, but all it does is make me prouder to be your husband, to be with the woman who's loved me all these years. But I'm the same, and I love you the same. I want to celebrate with *you*, not with anyone else."

He held their joined hands up in front of him, and Shelly stepped back, still sniffling. "So are we going to hit the movie theater? I'm thinking the art house, something with subtitles." She blushed, because there was that one time when he got down on his knees, not an easy task for a man pushing 280 pounds, and planted his face between her legs. He was doing it because he loved giving head, but also because he knew how loud she usually got when she was close to orgasm. He was throwing down a dare, a challenge that would either make her come or get them kicked out. She loved that he was willing to take such a risk.

"We're just gonna leave everyone?"

"Leave it to me," he said, and then took his hand and wrapped it around her wrist. It was still big enough to encircle her there, and she felt the breath whoosh from her body, the blood circle below her waist. She went to get her coat.

She smiled at a neighbor who gave her a quizzical look and didn't try to answer anyone's questions as Ron hustled her into his car. "I left Katie in charge; she's good at that sort of thing." Their friend was, indeed, the type who could problem-solve her way out of most any situation. Shelly relaxed against the seat and as Ron drove, his hand wandered to her lap. She reached for it, staring down at their entwined hands, his slightly tanner than hers.

They didn't speak during the twenty-minute drive, and she moved as if on autopilot. This wasn't the way the afternoon was supposed to go, but she knew they needed it. She especially knew it when, after giving the clerk their ticket order, Ron leaned over and whispered, "Take off your panties and give them to me."

She didn't protest, though she did hurry inside and use the bathroom to perform the task. She slipped him the balled-up red mesh and instead of simply tucking it into his pocket, he made a show of slowly letting the fabric flutter loose, just enough for Shelly to stare at him in horror, to look around in an exaggeratedly slow way, to catch his devilish smile in return. "What are we seeing?" she asked, even though she didn't really care.

She didn't know the film or the director or the language. Subtitles weren't really her thing, but they weren't really here for the story. At least, not that story. Shelly wasn't there to eat Twizzlers or popcorn or drink Diet Coke either, but she let Ron buy them for her, and let him put his hand on her ass while she carried the soda and Twizzlers.

But it wasn't until the lights went down that Shelly truly relaxed. She felt herself sink into the seat; this time they were near the wall, with her closest and Ron beside her. He'd made sure to pick a row that wasn't crowded, and he put the popcorn on his other side, then opened the Twizzlers and fed one to her. She smiled at him as she chewed the licorice while he held it, until she reached his fingers. She licked them gently, enjoying his soft moan, feeling almost giddy at having run off in the middle of their own party to play at being luststruck. Or maybe they weren't playing at all, because when he reached for her hand with his free one and held it, she felt nothing but love and lust coursing through her.

"I'm always going to be here for you," he whispered in her ear, so softly that had her hearing not been as sharp as it was, she might have missed it. She felt a tear roll down her cheek and brushed it away, not wanting to ruin the moment. He took her hand and guided it up under her sundress, the one she'd bought at their local thrift store, the one he'd said made her look like a sexy housewife. They'd both laughed, because she was the chief breadwinner in their home, designing websites and doing consulting while he wrote plays and taught at the local university. But still, she thought of it as her slutty housewife dress, and reaching under its red and white polka-dotted hem to touch her bare pussy, with his hand atop hers, was exquisite. She couldn't remember the last time she'd used her fingers on herself, certainly not going slow and sensual like this. Usually it was a quickie with her plug-in vibrator and she was lucky if she could focus on it. Usually she was on all fours, and she loved that, but they hadn't made love in any sense of the phrase in a long, long time. Fucking was one thing, a wonderful thing, but she'd missed this.

"I want to feel you," he whispered, again, so soft, so tender, and both of their fingers pressed inside her, two of hers, two of his. His thumb managed to find her clit and she forced herself not to lock her legs tight, to stay loose and open, all while trying to look at the screen and produce some semblance of the same laughs or groans as were coming from the other audience members. Thankfully the film had a loud rock soundtrack, because even with her biting her lip, Shelly couldn't keep from making noise. Ron's hand, the hand she'd fantasized about holding, was suddenly over her mouth, his fingers inside her overtaking hers. She let her wet fingers drop to her side and he became the king of her body, the invading conqueror intent on his prize. She curled her hand around the seat and this time looked down, watching in the dim light as he pushed and twisted inside her, watching as he crouched halfway down, not caring who saw as he silently but swiftly worked his manual magic on her cunt.

Soon she was shaking, squeezing him tight, closing her eyes as she focused purely on the sensation of her husband, her he-man, her true love giving her something no one, not even she, could. This was no longer about the girls at the party, or his weight, or even him proving himself to her. It was a reminder that they'd neglected this side of their relationship for too long, and the orgasm that shook through Shelly made her feel like she'd never come before in her life, not like that. And after, when Ron kept his fingers inside her, insisting they stay for the whole movie, even though she was desperate to go, desperate to see him fully, to pay proper homage to every inch of him, the new muscles and the old favorites, they sat there, with three fingers of his left hand gently inside her, and his right holding hers until the lights came up.

STORM SURGE

Teresa Noelle Roberts

The Bourne Bridge is going to be hell," Mark said from the passenger seat, looking at the westbound lane of Route 6. "It looked bad when we came over and the sheeple are leaving in droves." We were one of only a few cars heading out toward the eastern end of Cape Cod. A steady, sluggishly advancing stream was inching toward the mainland, though, headlights on against rain that was still light, but driven by fierce wind.

I sniffed scornfully. "What a bunch of wimps."

"Not everyone loves storms the very special way we do." Mark put his hand on my thigh. That was all he did, because I was driving and he didn't want to distract me too much, but it was enough to make me shudder with sudden need. The strangely lit sky, the fluctuating air pressure, the sense that something big was coming, all conspired either for or against me, depending on how you looked at it. My nerves were the kind of jangled where the wrong song on the radio might make me cry but even the lightest, most incidental touch from Mark might make me come. Mark knew I'd reached that point. I could tell by his smile when he added, "If they had someone like you with them, they'd stay."

I glanced again toward the snails'-pace eastbound traffic. "Sheesh, people have no sense of adventure. It's not even a hurricane, just a tropical storm, and it's supposed to brush by us without hitting land." I was mostly being tongue-in-cheek and Mark knew it. We knew that driving out to the family's summerhouse in the face of a major storm was potentially dangerous. While Tropical Storm Vic had much diminished from the Category 4 hurricane it had been when it roared to life in the Caribbean, its winds still packed a wallop and the predicted combination of heavy rain and storm-churned surf was the sort of thing that had been known to wash out huge stretches of Cape Cod beach, sometimes with homes still on them.

But Mark's folks' summerhouse was on a bluff overlooking the water, not at water level. It wasn't a guarantee, since Cape Cod bluffs were mostly sand, but it had survived the great hurricane of 1938 and every hurricane since, with a broken window here, the stairs to the beach washing out there, but no serious damage. We figured it was a fairly safe bet to survive a mere tropical storm.

It also had a bedroom with a queen-sized bed and huge windows opening onto an ocean view, pretty much the opposite of where a sensible couple would ride out a storm as bad as Vic threatened to be, but we never claimed to be sensible.

Sensual, sure. Sexual, decidedly. Sensible? We didn't go around licking live wires for kicks or anything, but we'd met in a kite-boarding seminar and connected when we both admitted, over lunch, that waves and wind that were almost too much to handle made us hot. On our second date we climbed Mount Washington, one of the more dangerous mountains in the continental

United States—and enjoyed a desperate, most-of-the-clothes-still-on quickie leaning on boulders at the top of the mountain, buffeted by the howling wind and just out of the sight of Mount Washington Observatory. (In case you're not a weather junkie, that's the home of the highest wind speed ever recorded. That day wasn't even close to a record, but you couldn't have convinced my raw, chapped face or incredibly wet pussy of that.)

You be the judge of how sensible we are.

Mark moved his hand and ran his fingers up my arm from the wrist to just past the elbow.

Sensation blasted through me like Vic had blasted through several islands on its way north. This was the good kind of devastation, but on a rain-slicked road, it could be just as dangerous as a tree crashing through the roof. I might play with the risk for a few seconds if it were just us, letting the sense of peril heighten my arousal like the storm did, but there were other people on the road. I shuddered, bit my lip and gripped the wheel until my knuckles were white. "Too sensitive," I managed to say. "Not while I'm driving."

"I think," Mark whispered, "that the storm's going to hit earlier than predicted."

He was right. By the time we rolled into the driveway of the cottage, the rain whipped sideways. Screaming wind almost drowned out the roaring, crashing surf.

We'd be soaked by the time we made it in the front door.

My shorts were already soaked.

In the driveway, I had to fight against the wind to move forward. Three steps before reaching the minimal shelter of the tiny porch, I clenched at the fierceness and grabbed Mark, pulled him close and kissed him with an intensity that rivaled the storm.

The wind had weight, and it pushed us closer together. It

smelled like the tropics and the rain was curiously warm.

Or maybe Mark and I were so heated the rain steamed on contact with our skin.

We'd been spurred on before by nor'easters and blizzards, made love during a violent thunderstorm on a deserted beach in Bermuda, snuck off together in the middle of a tornado warning (fortunately the tornadoes never materialized) while visiting friends in Illinois. But the thrill had never been so intense before, and the worst of Vic hadn't hit yet. Or would that be the best of Vic?

Mark grabbed my ass with both big hands, pulling me forward and grinding me against his straining cock. Inside, I was roaring and surging like the surf. His cock felt so rigid the wind might snap him if he weren't sheltered against my body.

The primal part of me that responded to danger and violent weather wanted to rush down to the beach with him, to tear our clothes off in full view of the storm, to see if the wild waves would tear us out to sea as we made love on the sand.

Unfortunately they were all too likely to do so. We were adrenaline junkies, but the only death that interested us was the classic old metaphor for orgasm. The actual stopping-of-heart-and-brain-function kind would spoil all our fun.

"Inside," Mark whispered, his breath hot in my ear and on my rain-slicked skin. "Can you imagine how much our friends would laugh if we blew away and were found floating in Provincetown Harbor or something?"

"At least we'd die happy. We'd probably fuck in midair."

"Which is why our friends would laugh. The Coast Guard would find us still locked together." He tugged on my hand. "Come on."

The old cottage was studiedly simple, as weathered-looking inside as it was outside, but sturdy. It had been built over a hundred years ago and had withstood many a storm before this one, but it still felt like a fragile shell determinedly protecting us from the seething weather outside. The power was still on, but that, too, seemed very fragile, almost as fragile as the remaining light did, dimmed by the storm. We grabbed an oil lamp from the center of the kitchen table and took it into the bedroom with us. Eventually, we'd need it.

I pushed the blue cotton curtains open. It wasn't easy to see much beside a gray wall of rain, but the roar of the surf was even stronger just from crossing the narrow width of the cottage and getting that much closer to the ocean.

Mark grabbed me from behind and pulled me sharply back against him. He'd already shucked his wet clothes and was deliciously hard. His damp skin was surface-chilled, but heat throbbed and pulsed underneath. "Why are you still dressed?" he asked, his voice as harsh and raw as the weather and even more thrilling. We aren't kinky, not in a BDSM sense—although our craving for big weather, erotic adrenaline rushes and risky places to screw must count as kinky—but I can't help responding when he gets rough and edgy because it means the situation's getting under his skin, too.

Before I could say anything, he'd yanked my shorts down, ruched my shirt up. He didn't even bother undressing me completely.

"Hang on to the windowsill and spread your legs," he said, half command, half plea.

I wriggled my shorts the rest of the way off; kicked the sodden things, along with my flip-flops, halfway across the room. I bent over, stuck my ass out, gazed out over the wild rain and churning ocean.

Mark was inside me in the time it took one line of crazy-big waves to break onto the beach below.

The waves had a rhythm, a mad crash followed by a roar like some prehistoric animal as the retreating mass of water dragged a layer of sand, shell and rock with it.

Mark set himself to follow that rhythm, slow but inexorable.

The wind had no rhythm, yet it did. It pulsed and throbbed and vibrated, but its pattern was either too fast or too slow for the human brain to make out.

The human cunt, or at least my cunt, understood it just fine. I clenched and arched to Mark's rhythm, the rhythm of the sea; but my blood, my mind, my desire was more like the wind: a force that surrounded, enveloped, controlled.

I needed more. Needed more of Mark. Needed more of the storm. "Open the window," I said in a way that Mark understood also meant, "Fuck me harder."

"Stand back."

Moving away from me with a small sound of regret and apology, he opened the latch on the casement window farthest from us. The old window blew back abruptly, propelled by wind and rain that had the force of a freight train. Mark caught the window before it crashed into the wall and shattered, letting out an "Oof," of discomfort as it smacked into his hands. Fighting the wind, he eased it back against the wall and hooked it open. The screen that remained in place bowed before the wind.

We moved closer to the force that was invading the house.

My hair whipped uncontrollably. The rain felt colder now, and driven by wind, it stung against my skin. The harsh sensation crinkled my nipples, sent more lust surging tidally through my body. The lust centered in my cunt, but it spiraled from there to fill my body like a hurricane spinning out from its eye. My cunt, though, was far from the eerie calm of a hurricane's eye. Wild with need, it clenched and gripped at nothing

Mark pushed me forward so my face and upper body were half out the window. With a wordless cry, he drove into me again, his cock as fierce as the storm. No longer following the crash of the surf, he fucked double time or faster, forcing my arousal so high I thought I'd soar out the window and ride the wind like an albatross. His hands gripped my hips as if by holding them so tightly, he kept us both from blowing away, or at least made sure we'd be carried off together. The bruising force of his fingers played against the primal forces of wind and water and his equally primal cock took me over completely.

Surf-noise and the howling wind surrounded us. Rain drenched us, chilling and heating us at the same time. I heard a different pounding, a different roaring: my heart racing with fear and arousal, my blood pumping through my veins, spurred by a crazy cocktail of danger and desire.

There was nothing else left, just Mark and Tropical Storm Vic. The waves, as huge as they were, broke well below the house, but if a rogue wave took out the house and we were dragged out to sea, I wouldn't have cared as long as the ocean kept Mark and me locked together until we drowned.

I came surging like the ocean, came howling like the wind, came squirting all over Mark and the already wet wooden floor so I added my own moisture to the rain. Mark roared a noise as untamed and beautiful and fierce as Vic's passionate cries and surged into my convulsing cunt.

We sank to the floor, too spent to make it to the bed. The rain drenched us as we lay there so it felt like the wild ocean had invaded the house. "Best ever," Mark whispered in my ear. "Love you, babe. But how can we top this?"

"Category 5 hurricane on one of those little Caribbean islands that almost gets washed off the map every time a good blow hits, maybe. Or we take up tornado chasing and screw in some Midwestern pasture while the sky turns green and the funnel cloud gets closer and closer." I sighed and snuggled closer.

"We could be a new Weather Channel series: 'The Storm Fuckers.' They'd have to put us on late at night, though."

"I guess they're both bad ideas," I reluctantly conceded. "And taking your dad's boat out in this would be an even stupider one. Hot, but stupid." I didn't need to tell Mark that just thinking of these insane ideas had set lust surging again, even if they were too dangerous to ever carry out.

I didn't need to tell him because his cock had quickened and thickened despite his recent orgasm. He understood me.

"If we lived through it, Dad would kill us. Besides, he had the boat pulled from the marina and moved to higher ground when the storm warnings started coming in. But you know what is a good idea?"

I shook my head.

"Fighting the window shut before the floor gets totally ruined, then going to bed to watch and listen. I bet the power's going out any time now. Might as well get cozy." The way he said *get cozy* definitely meant *fuck like lust-crazed beasts*.

As if he'd cut the line with his words, the lights went out.

In the near darkness, the rush of wind and wave, the sense of being overpowered by nature became even more intense.

And my personal storm surged with it. "Great idea," I said. "But hurry."

UNDERCOVER KINK

Louisa Harte

I stroll down the street in my smart office suit, smiling at the teasing pull of my PVC panties between my legs. I love wearing kinky underwear. From the seductive grip of a stocking around my thigh to the slick press of latex panties over my pussy, it's become an obsession.

Escapism or risqué rebellion—I don't care what the psychology is, it's an essential part of my kink. Hidden beneath my conservative office clothes, it's my horny secret. At home alone in my flat, there's nothing I like better than cranking up the stereo and stripping down to my undies to act out my dreams. Music pumping, I dance in front of the mirror and play with my pussy, imagining others watching me. It's my favorite fantasy. It never fails to get me off.

Time to get some more goodies.

Reaching the department store, I push open the door and head to the lingerie department. Scantily clad mannequins line the aisles. With their painted smiles, it's as if they know they're kitted out in the city's hottest lingerie. I don't need convincing— I save my paycheck for this monthly treat. I browse the racks of colorful clothing; just being around them feels intoxicating. I run my fingers over the sexy fabrics. There are outfits to suit all tastes, from virginal to slutty.

Today, it's the latter look I'm after.

I head to the counter, looking for Chantal, the lingerie manager. Flamboyant and sexy, with her intimate knowledge of lingerie she's become a good friend, offering me advice on the latest designs. But today she's nowhere to be seen.

Instead, standing at the counter is a tall, hunky guy. With cropped black hair and intense brown eyes, he's quite a looker. Even the store's simple uniform looks hot on his athletic physique. But it's his eyes that grab me most. Liquid brown, they seem to bore right into me. "Hi. I'm Brad," he says. "Can I help you?"

I stand there, his eyes pinning me to the spot. Then I realize he's waiting for a response. "Oh, sorry. I'm Natalie. I'm looking for Chantal?"

"She's just gone out." He sweeps his gaze over my body, giving me a particularly thorough once-over. "I'm covering for her."

"Right." I nod, trying to keep my composure. He seems a bit out of place in this department. Still, he adds a brawny appeal. And those eyes...

"Anyway, how can I help you?" he prompts.

"Chantal's ordered an outfit for me?"

"An outfit?" Brad raises a brow.

"A basque," I explain. Somehow, just saying the word to Brad gives it a new edge.

Brad cocks his head. "Can you describe it?"

Is he toying with me? My cheeks flush; I'm not normally this coy. I stare into his brown eyes and answer as calmly as I can. "It's red latex."

The corner of Brad's mouth quirks up. "Yes..."

"With lace trim cups."

Without a trace of reticence, Brad's gaze dips to my breasts. He smiles. "Come to think of it, I do know which one you mean." Like a magician producing a rabbit from a hat, he reaches under the counter and immediately pulls out a basque. "With lace-up front for easy access," he muses, examining the label. "That's handy..."

The flush on my face ramps up a notch. He's enjoying this, I can tell.

"Was there anything else to go with that?" he asks.

"Um, a pair of stockings," I mutter.

Brad tilts his head.

Here we go again. "Red fishnet stockings," I say quietly, surprised at how bashful I've become.

"Kinky." Brad reaches under the counter again and pulls out the stockings, laying them down on the desk. I stare down at the slutty outfit. It's right up my alley—my nipples harden just looking at it.

"So, are you gonna try these on?" Brad asks.

I scoop the kinky garments to my chest and meet his gaze. "Of course I am."

There's a definite twinkle in his eye as he strides out from behind the counter and leads me to the changing room. Even though I know the way like the back of my hand, it's like he's got this hold over me, and I teeter after him, trying to keep pace with his strides. Brad opens the dressing room door and gestures me through.

I step into the room with its mirrored walls and plush inte-rior. I always feel like a princess when I come to this store, and today, with Brad here, it feels like I've got my own personal prince, too. Laying the outfit over a chair, I turn around to face him. "Okay, thanks," I say.

Brad leans in the doorway, seeming reluctant to move. "Shout up if you need anything," he says. But he still doesn't move. He just stands there, watching me in the mirror.

My skin prickles at his scrutiny. And not in a bad way.

Finally, with a lingering glance, Brad closes the door and leaves.

Taking a breath, I get down to business and strip down to my red PVC panties. I pick up the basque and run my fingers over the shiny latex. I love it: the color, the shape, the slick, rubbery feel of it. I hold it against my chest. It's a perfect match with my knickers. Enough of the admiring—time to try it on. I squeeze myself into the sexy basque, enjoying the way the latex molds to my skin. As I lace up the front, the material presses against my nipples and spills a glimpse of my tits over the top. I grin. I've come a long way from the geeky kid with puppy fat. Now I've got curves in all the right places and they sure feel hot packed into this killer outfit.

There's a knock at the door.

"Yeah?" I holler.

"Everything okay in there?"

It sounds like Brad.

I glance at myself in the mirror, my voluptuous body squeezed into the raunchy basque. A rush of adrenaline pumps through me. "I wouldn't mind a second opinion..." My hand flies to my mouth, but the words are out before I can stop them.

The door opens and I feel a moment of panic. *What the hell am I doing?* But this is no time for questions. Brad stands in the doorway, his cocky smile fading as he stares at my scantily clad body. "Wow, you look hot," he says.

Shock gives way to pleasure and I catch his gaze in the mirror. "You think so?"

Brad ogles my tits wrestling against the front of the basque. "Yeah, I think so." Slowly, Brad shifts his gaze to the skimpy panties hugging my ass and then down to my thighs. "But there's something missing..."

Our eyes meet in the mirror. His gaze flicks to the stockings lying over the chair, then back to me.

A subtle directive.

I hesitate, filled with conflicting emotions. But excitement gets the better of me and I bend over to pick up the stockings, my tight PVC panties stretching over my ass, emphasizing the full curve of my buttocks. As I scoop up the stockings, the gusset of my knickers pulls tightly over my pussy. I lift my gaze to the mirror to see Brad watching my every move. My panties suddenly feel slippery. Brad's watchful eyes are turning me on.

What the hell have I got myself into?

But it's too late to back out now and I straighten up and turn the chair toward me. Propping first one foot, then the other on the seat, I glide the fishnet stockings up over my legs. Brad's gaze is so hot, I can almost feel it burning my skin. His eyes flick from the mirror to me as I clip the basque's garter straps to the tops of the stockings. My panties grow wetter. I've never been watched so intimately before. Smoothing my hands up over my stockings, I glance over my shoulder to look at him. "Is that better?" I ask coyly.

"You bet." Brad leans against the doorframe like he could stand and watch me all day.

A few moments pass. "Shouldn't you be serving?" I can hear the reluctance in my voice.

Brad's eyes darken. "Forget the other customers. You've got my attention."

I feel my power surge between us, tethering his gaze to the mirror. I glance down to see a bulge developing in his trousers.

"Come here," he whispers.

Instinctively, I step backward and push my panty-clad ass up against his crotch. "Like this?" I ask. My voice is barely a whisper.

"Yeah, like that." Brad's hands flinch by his sides as his eyes rove over my body. "But I want to see more..."

"Like what?"

Brad leans closer and whispers against my ear. "Surprise me."

My heart pounds. I've imagined flaunting my body for some hot horny stranger a thousand times alone, at home in my flat. But can I do it for real? And here? Somehow, I don't think I've got the nerve. "I can't," I say.

Brad kicks the door shut and flips the lock. "Sure you can." He pulls up a chair and settles back into it. He eyes me hungrily like he expects a good show.

The two sides of my psyche wrestle in my head, and I shift my gaze to the mirror. The sight of myself transformed by this kinky outfit gives me a sudden rush of courage. This is my chance to have fun.

"Okay. You asked for it." I stand in front of Brad and close my eyes. In my head I hear the music begin to play—silent beats electrify my mind and move my body. I flick open my eyes and begin to dance to the rhythm, gyrating my hips, moving closer to Brad.

Brad leans forward, drinking in my movements with his eyes. I grind my pelvis in slow circles, moving my body up and down, awakening my inner slut. It's surprisingly easy once I get started. Sliding my hands seductively over my body, I run my fingers over the shiny basque, squeezing my breasts through the slippery fabric. *Damn, this feels good.* I shimmy closer, bucking my hips like a private dancer. Spurred on by Brad's lustful expression, I slowly unlace the basque, parting the latex to reveal a glimpse of my breasts. Brad swallows, his eyes wide, expectant.

I glance at myself in the mirror. Seeing myself dancing so provocatively turns me on, but it's the filthy look in Brad's eyes that drives me on even more. Inching closer, I push open his thighs and gyrate sexily between them. Brad skims his hands up over my waist, reaching to cup my latex-covered tits.

"No touching," I scold. In a swift movement, I whip the tie from around his neck and place it over his wrists, binding his hands together behind his back. "You didn't expect that, did you?" Truth be told, neither did I. This scenario is bringing out a totally new side of me.

Brad wrenches against the tie, his eyes lusty. I lean forward and push my cleavage into his face. Brad moans. His breath tickles my skin and I close my eyes, enjoying the sensation. *Never take your eyes off the audience.* I flick my eyes open as, without warning, Brad catches the lace ties between his teeth and tugs. The basque peels open, spilling my tits into his face. Moving quickly, he catches a nipple in his mouth.

"Naughty," I chastise, but my nipple doesn't seem to think it's naughty at all. In fact my other nipple wants some of it, too. I take a step back and try to remember that this is a striptease and that *I'm* the one who's supposed to be in charge.

"You bloody tease," Brad groans.

"That's the idea," I say, as much to remind myself as him. My panties grow creamy. If I'm not careful, I might cross the line. *If there is one.*

Brad drops his gaze to my knickers. "Take 'em off," he mutters.

"What?"

"Take 'em off," he repeats, slowly, deliberately.

Turning my back to him, I bend over and slide the tight PVC knickers down over my ass. Brad groans as I push the slick scrap of material down over my stocking-clad thighs to my ankles. Stepping out of them, I kick them aside and turn around to face him.

Brad's gaze is electric "Are you wet?" he murmurs.

Spurred on by his question, I dip a finger into my pussy. I smile, my voice low and husky. "For you, honey, I'm soaking."

Brad groans. "Let me taste you."

"You can't," I tease. I slide my finger seductively over my clit. "You're just here to watch..."

My words seem to drive him crazy. Brad tugs against the tie. "Fine...then make yourself come," he rasps.

His words are like music to my ears. If this scenario was horny in my imagination, it's even hornier in reality. I climb onto his lap, my tits brushing against his chest. Brad's eyes sparkle, encouraging me. Sliding my hand between my thighs, I stifle a moan as I begin to wank myself off.

I hear Brad's heart racing beneath his shirt as I rub my clit. Knowing he's turned on by my performance only makes me hotter. I gaze in the mirror, watching Brad watching me, my whole body buzzing as I bring myself off for this sexy stranger in the middle of the lingerie department.

It doesn't get any better than this.

Only it does. There's a click next door as someone enters the changing room next to ours. I glance at Brad. He smiles, a wicked gleam in his eyes.

That does it. I rub my clit faster, trying to stifle my gasps, but the added thrill of someone listening next door sends me over the edge. Grasping Brad's shoulders, I groan as the orgasm hits.

I arch my back as shudders reverberate through me, spilling like waves through my body.

Gradually coming back to my senses, I look down to see Brad still watching me, his face contorted into a mask of pleasure and pain. I slide my hand to his crotch. The erection in his pants feels set to explode. I smile at his pained expression and the heat flooding my body. I should feel sated. I've had my fun; I've acted out my fantasy with blissful abandon. But somehow it's not enough.

Our gazes meet. There's a moment's pause. Then Brad whispers against my ear, "Now fuck me."

All is silent next door, like our secret audience is holding an anticipatory breath. I don't waste a moment. The sound echoes off the walls as I pull down Brad's zipper. He clamps his lips together as I take out his cock. And it's a big one. Straddling his thighs, I hold his thick shaft in my hand, delighting in the feel of it. Shiny latex and a huge hard cock all in one day—*I am a lucky girl.*

Placing my hands on his chest, I sink down onto his shaft, burying it inch by inch into my cunt. I almost squeal with excitement; it feels so naughty, filling my greedy pussy with this stranger's hot prick. Brad grits his teeth, his expression hungry as I start to pump him. Moving faster, I shift my gaze to the mirror, watching wide-eyed as I fuck him. My pussy pulses in response to the view. I've never felt so horny in my life.

As I slam down onto him, I'm sure I hear a sigh from next door. The thought of our clandestine listener makes me bang him even harder. Brad groans with delight. We heave and buck, the chair creaking, our groans mingling in a hot, sweaty rush of sex. I rub myself against him, feeling another climax building inside me. I'm powerless to stop it as it hits me with force, rolling through my belly and exploding in my pussy. Grasping a handful of Brad's hair, I come hard on his lap, grinding down onto him in ecstasy.

"Oh, hell!" Brad suddenly breaks free of his binds to clutch at my ass. His hands holding me still, his cock quivers as he comes deep inside me. He groans, his cock pulsing, my pussy happily milking all that he's got.

After a few blissful moments, Brad leans against me, breathless. He tips his head, his eyes glassy. "You bloody slut," he teases.

I press my lips against his ear. "You asked for it."

Brad gives me a cheeky smile. "Yeah, I suppose I did."

A knock at the door interrupts. *"Brad? Are you in there?"* a voice calls.

Brad turns his head. "Who is it?"

"Chantal."

Shit. I gaze into the mirror at our shameless display: me sitting pantyless astride Brad in the fishnet stockings, the expensive basque hanging open, my tits in his face.

We're in for it now.

"I'll just be a minute, Chantal," Brad mutters. Reluctantly, we pry ourselves apart. Peeling off the outfit, I tug on my clothes while Brad zips up his trousers, tosses his tie around his neck and strides to the door to unlock it. I sigh, realizing my fantasy has come to an end. Picking up the basque and stockings, I turn to follow him. But as I reach the door, he blocks my way, his expression serious. "That was some show you put on there," he says softly.

Pleasure flutters in my belly. "You think so?"

Brad leans in and gives me a hard, unapologetic kiss in reply.

My senses are still reeling when Chantal's voice calls out again. "I'll be over at the counter, Brad."

Brad gives me a last, lingering look, then opens the door and strides away to the counter. As I stand in the doorway, watching him go, a woman steps out of the changing room next to ours. Catching my eye, she gives me a complicit smile before disappearing off into the store. I swallow, clutching the undies to my chest. *Were we that obvious? Oh, hell. Time to face the music.*

Over at the counter, Chantal seems to be giving Brad a grilling. My stomach tightens. She must know. That's me banned for life and him sacked. And all because I had to get off!

I rush over to join them. "Chantal, it's my fault," I say.

Chantal turns to me and smiles. "Hey, Natalie, good to see you."

"Brad was just giving me some...assistance," I continue, trying to come up with a plausible excuse.

"Of course he was," says Chantal, a strangely complacent look on her face.

I lay the basque and stockings down on the counter, attempting to act normal. "Anyway, I'll take these, please."

"Great choice." Chantal nods. "I promised you something special, didn't I?"

I gaze down at the kinky outfit, my body still zinging from the steamy encounter. "Yeah, it's great," I murmur.

"Something I thought would suit you..." Chantal continues.

I lift my head to see her glance purposely at Brad. I follow her gaze. Brad shoves his hands into his pockets and gives me a shifty smile. "Right ladies, I think I'd better be off," he mumbles.

I glance back at Chantal. She's stifling a smile. My brows furrow as I flick my gaze between the two of them. My mouth falls open. *I've been set up!* Chantal's the only one who knows about my kinky clothing obsession.

Shaking my head, I try to take it all in. I should feel angry, but as Brad turns to leave, I feel a sudden sense of loss. I've just had the hottest sex of my life thanks to him and it's not something I'm ready to let go of. Not yet.

"Hey, Brad!" I call.

Brad turns around and fixes me with those intense brown eyes.

I tip my head coyly. "If I ever need a second opinion..."

Brad gives me a smile. "You got it."

I scoop up my undies and head out of the store. Somehow I don't think I can wait another month for my next visit.

ABOUT THE AUTHORS

BELLA ANDRE (BellaAndre.com) writes "sensual, empowered stories enveloped in heady romance" (*Publisher's Weekly*) about sizzling alpha heroes and the strong women they'll love forever. Her books have been *Cosmopolitan* Red Hot Reads twice and have been translated into German, Thai, Japanese and Ukrainian.

LOGAN BELLE went to her first burlesque show on her birthday two years ago and has been following the scene and writing about it ever since. Her debut erotic novel is *Blue Angel*, the first in a series. Her short fiction has appeared on Oysters & Chocolate. She lives in New York City. Read more at loganbelle.com.

ELIZABETH COLDWELL lives and writes in London. Her work has appeared in a number of Cleis anthologies including *Please, Sir*; *Fast Girls*; *Bottoms Up* and *Naked*.

PORTIA DA COSTA pens both romance and women's erotica and is the author of over twenty novels and a hundred-plus short stories. Praised for her vivid, emotional writing, she's best known for her Black Lace titles, but now writes for a variety of publishers, including Harlequin Spice and Samhain.

With coauthors and on her own, **ANDREA DALE** has sold two novels to Virgin Books UK and approximately 100 stories to Harlequin Spice, Avon Red and Cleis Press, among others. All she can say about her inspiration for this story is "Mm, tattoos..." Her website is at cyvarwydd.com.

JUSTINE ELYOT has contributed to a plethora of anthologies from Black Lace, Cleis Press, Constable & Robinson and Xcite Books, and is the author of the Black Lace title *On Demand*. More recently, she has been writing erotic romance novellas, which are available from Total E-Bound.

EMERALD's erotic fiction has been published in anthologies edited by Violet Blue, Rachel Kramer Bussel, Jolie du Pre, and Alison Tyler as well as at various erotic websites. She lives in Maryland and serves as an activist for reproductive freedom and sex worker rights. Find her online at thegreenlightdistrict.org.

K. D. GRACE lives in England with her husband. She is passionate about nature, writing and sex—not necessarily in that order. Her novel, *The Initiation of Ms. Holly*, was published by Xcite Books.

ARIEL GRAHAM lives, writes and entertains her own obsessions in northern Nevada with her husband who is also her best friend, and her own deeply suspicious cats. Her work can be found in anthologies including *Please, Sir; Please, Ma'am; Afternoon Delight: Erotica for Couples* and in various web-based magazines.

LOUISA HARTE's erotic fiction appears in the Cleis Press anthologies *Best Women's Erotica 2010* and *2011; Fairy Tale Lust; Orgasmic: Erotica for Women* and *Smooth: Erotic Stories for Women.* Currently living in New Zealand, she finds inspiration from many places, including her thoughts, dreams and fantasies. Visit her at louisaharte.com.

ADELE HAZE writes sexy stories because she doesn't know how not to. When she isn't writing fiction, she tries to educate the world about sex-positive attitudes, female gaze in erotic arts, and acceptance of sexual preferences of others. For the rest of the time, she models for BDSM erotica.

KAYLA PERRIN (kaylaperrin.com) is a multi-published *USA Today* and *Essence*® bestselling author with thirty-six books in print. She is published in a variety of genres, including mystery/suspense, romance and mainstream fiction. She has been featured on "Entertainment Tonight Canada," *Who's Afraid of Happy Endings* (Bravo documentary about the romance genre) and "A.M. Buffalo."

JENNIFER PETERS has a lot of obsessions, including avocados, music, books and everything kitsch. When she's not obsessing about the finer things in life, she's a completely neurotic writer and editor for the *Penthouse* magazine group, where she obsesses over porn and punctuation, in that order. Her stories can be found in *Peep Show, Fast Girls, Smooth, Best Bondage Erotica 2011* and *Gotta Have It.*

CARIDAD PIÑEIRO is the *New York Times*–bestselling author of over twenty-five paranormal romance and romantic suspense novels and novellas. Her popular *The Calling* vampire series returns in 2012 and look for *The Lost*, the latest release in the acclaimed *Sin Hunter* series. For more information on Caridad, please visit caridad.com.

TERESA NOELLE ROBERTS's short fiction has appeared in numerous anthologies, including *Sweet Love: Erotic Fantasies for Couples, Orgasmic, Dirty Girls* and *Best of Best Women's Erotica 2*. She also writes erotic romance for several publishers. Disclaimer: author is not liable for injuries incurred under the influence of this story.

CHARLOTTE STEIN has published many stories in various erotic anthologies as well as her own collection of short stories, *The Things That Make Me Give In*. She has novellas and a novel with Ellora's Cave, Total-E-Bound and Xcite, and you can contact her at themightycharlottestein.blogspot.com.

DONNA GEORGE STOREY believes a kiss is worth a thousand words. She is the author of *Amorous Woman*, a steamy tale of an American woman's love affair with Japan, as well as many short stories, which have appeared in *Best Women's Erotica, Penthouse, Fast Girl,* and *Passion*. Read more at DonnaGeorgeStorey.com.

GARNELL WALLACE has been spellbound by love stories ever since she read her first one as a teenager. She is hard at work on her own addition to this continually evolving and enduring genre. She can be reached at myspace.com/garnellwallace.

KRISTINA WRIGHT (kristinawright.com) lives in Virginia with her husband Jay and her son Patrick. She is the editor of the anthologies *Fairy Tale Lust* and *Demon Lover* and her short fiction has appeared in over eighty anthologies. She holds degrees in English and humanities and teaches college-level composition and mythology.

ABOUT
THE EDITOR

RACHEL KRAMER BUSSEL (rachelkramerbussel.com) is a New York–based author, editor and blogger. She has edited over thirty books of erotica, including *Gotta Have It; Best Bondage Erotica 2011; Surrender; Orgasmic; Bottoms Up: Spanking Good Stories; Spanked; Naughty Spanking Stories from A to Z 1* and *2; Fast Girls; Smooth; Passion; The Mile High Club; Do Not Disturb; Tasting Him; Tasting Her; Please, Sir; Please, Ma'am; He's on Top; She's on Top; Caught Looking; Hide and Seek; Crossdressing* and *Rubber Sex*. She is the author of the forthcoming novel, *Everything But...*, and the nonfiction book, *How To Write an Erotic Love Letter, Best Sex Writing* series editor, and winner of 5 IPPY (Independent Publisher) Awards. Her work has been published in over one hundred anthologies, including *Best American Erotica 2004* and *2006; Zane's Chocolate Flava 2* and *Purple Panties; Everything You Know About Sex Is Wrong; Single State of the Union* and *Desire: Women Write About Wanting*. She serves as senior editor at *Penthouse*

Variation, and wrote the popular "Lusty Lady" column for the *Village Voice.*

Rachel is a sex columnist for SexisMagazine.com and has written for *AVN, Bust,* Cleansheets.com, *Cosmopolitan, Curve,* The Daily Beast, Fresh Yarn, TheFrisky.com, Gothamist, Huffington Post, Mediabistro, *Newsday, New York Post, Penthouse, Playgirl, Radar, San Francisco Chronicle, Time Out New York* and *Zink,* among others. She has appeared on "The Martha Stewart Show," "The Berman and Berman Show," NY1 and Showtime's "Family Business." She hosted the popular In the Flesh Erotic Reading Series (inthefleshreadingseries.com), featuring readers from Susie Bright to Zane, and speaks at conferences, does readings and teaches erotic writing workshops across the country. She blogs at lustylady.blogspot.com.

Find out more about *Obsessed* and the contributors at obsessederoticromance.com.

More from Rachel Kramer Bussel

Passion
Erotic Romance for Women
Edited by Rachel Kramer Bussel

Combining rich and explicit imagery with classic love stories, the best writers of erotic romance bring to life tales that can be read aloud in bed.
ISBN 978-1-57344-415-6 $14.95

Bottoms Up
Spanking Good Stories
Edited by Rachel Kramer Bussel

As sweet as it is kinky, *Bottoms Up* will propel you to pick up a paddle and share in both pleasure and pain, or perhaps simply turn the other cheek.
ISBN 978-1-57344-362-3 $14.95

Orgasmic
Erotica for Women
Edited by Rachel Kramer Bussel

What gets you off? Let *Orgasmic* count the ways...with 25 stories focused on female orgasm, there is something here for every reader.
ISBN 978-1-57344-402-6 $14.95

Please, Sir
Erotic Stories of Female Submission
Edited by Rachel Kramer Bussel

These 22 kinky stories celebrate the thrill of submission by women who know exactly what they want.
ISBN 978-1-57344-389-0 $14.95

Fast Girls
Erotica for Women
Edited by Rachel Kramer Bussel

Fast Girls celebrates the girl with a reputation, the girl who goes all the way, and the girl who doesn't know how to say "no."
ISBN 978-1-57344-384-5 $14.95

Out of This World Romance

Steamlust
Steampunk Erotic Romance
Edited by Kristina Wright

Shiny brass and crushed velvet; mechanical inventions and romantic conventions; sexual fantasy and kinky fetish: this is a lush and fantastical world of women-centered stories and romantic scenarios, a first for steampunk fiction.
ISBN 978-1-57344-721-8 $14.95

The Sweetest Kiss
Ravishing Vampire Erotica
Edited by D.L. King

These sanguine tales give new meaning to the term "dead sexy" and feature beautiful bloodsuckers whose desires go far beyond blood.
ISBN 978-1-57344-371-5 $15.95

Dream Lover
Paranormal Tales of Erotic Romance
Edited by Kristina Wright

A potent potion of fun and sexy tales filled with male fairies and clairvoyant scientists, as well as darkly erotic tales of ghosts, shapeshifters and possession.
ISBN 978-1-57344-655-6 $14.95

Fairy Tale Lust
Erotic Fantasies for Women
Edited by Kristina Wright

Award-winning novelist and erotica writer Kristina Wright goes over the river and through the woods to find the sexiest fairy tales ever written.
ISBN 978-1-57344-397-5 $14.95

In Sleeping Beauty's Bed
Erotic Fairy Tales
By Mitzi Szereto

"Who can resist the erotic origins of fairy tales from Little Red to Rapunzel's long braid? Szereto knows her way around the mythic scholarship and the most outrageous sexual deviations in Pandora's Box." —Susie Bright
ISBN 978-1-57344-367-8 $16.95

Ordering is easy! Call us toll free or fax us to place your MC/VISA order.
You can also mail the order form below with payment to:
Cleis Press, 2246 Sixth St., Berkeley, CA 94710.

ORDER FORM

QTY	TITLE	PRICE
_____	_____	_____
_____	_____	_____
_____	_____	_____
_____	_____	_____
_____	_____	_____
_____	_____	_____
_____	_____	_____
_____	_____	_____

SUBTOTAL	_____
SHIPPING	_____
SALES TAX	_____
TOTAL	_____

Add $3.95 postage/handling for the first book ordered and $1.00 for each additional book. Outside North America, please contact us for shipping rates. California residents add 8.75% sales tax. Payment in U.S. dollars only.

* Free book of equal or lesser value. Shipping and applicable sales tax extra.

Cleis Press • Phone: (800) 780-2279 • Fax: (510) 845-8001
orders@cleispress.com • www.cleispress.com
You'll find more great books on our website

Follow us on Twitter @cleispress • Friend/fan us on Facebook